Captivating story

Perfect for fans of
Jacqueline Wilson

...s well as being a writer,
Jess Bright is a DJ!

'I loved Sister, Sister
- it was the best book ever!'
Danni, aged 10

How far would
you go to save
your sister?

Here's a taste of what's to come...

Willow tried to imagine how the meeting would go; what Anthony would say. Would he be like Darth Vader in *The Empire Strikes Back* and say, 'Willow, I am your father; you have a sister,' in a very dramatic way, even though she knew all that already? What would he be like? Would he be a cool and trendy dad or one of those sad dads who looked as though they got dressed in the dark? Yes, Mum looked as though she was in a reality TV show called *When Clothes Attack*, but somehow, she wore it well. Mess, chaos, mismatching colours were part of her. Plus she was still very pretty for an ancient grown-up. It hadn't escaped Willow's attention that male teachers and some of the dads at school went bright red when talking to her mum. Mum, being Mum, was oblivious, though. Willow wondered if her mum had ever had a secret boyfriend.

She lay in bed replaying different scenarios and conversations in her head, and even imagining different dads. What if it was obvious Anthony really had no intention of being a dad, and all he was after was her bone marrow? What would she do then? Could she just walk away? Willow tossed and turned until the early hours, unable to sleep. She just wanted the truth to finally be revealed...

Hello there,

Families are weird, aren't they? I mean, here you are, all lumped together under one roof, and you're just supposed to get on without falling out or getting into major trouble. It's never, EVER going to be perfect!

Falling out and bickering with brothers and sisters is part of life. But Willow doesn't know how she's ever going to get Bella to accept her.

My experience in life and families is you can't force anything. Things always work out in the end. And if they don't, perhaps you're lucky enough to have a best friend like Willow does, who will help you to see things differently.

Love Jess

I would like to dedicate this book to my brother and sisters. First there was Pete, who grew up with me during the bad perm era. And then, years later, there came two extra surprises: Katie and Joanna. Our family is mad like all the others, but life would be so boring without you all. Especially after the Rugby Sevens and the Clapham Junction Platform Incident. That will make me laugh until I am an old lady!

OXFORD
UNIVERSITY PRESS

Great Clarendon Street, Oxford OX2 6DP
Oxford University Press is a department of the University of Oxford.
It furthers the University's objective of excellence in research, scholarship,
and education by publishing worldwide. Oxford is a registered trade mark of
Oxford University Press in the UK and in certain other countries

Database right Oxford University Press (maker)

First published 2015

British Library Cataloguing in Publication Data
Data available

ISBN: 978-0-19-273813-4

1 3 5 7 9 10 8 6 4 2
Printed in Great Britain

Paper used in the production of this book is a natural,
recyclable product made from wood grown in sustainable forests.
The manufacturing process conforms to the environmental
regulations of the country of origin.

SISTER, SISTER

Jess Bright

OXFORD
UNIVERSITY PRESS

Chapter One
Mystery letters

Willow pressed her nose up against the window of the school bus and breathed in the metallic whiff of wet glass. She wondered if there was going to be one of those letters waiting on the doormat when she got home after school this afternoon. Her heart sank each time she saw one. Mum would refuse to talk and stomp around the house in a worrying black mood every time one arrived. Willow wondered how such an innocuous cream envelope could harbour such a lot of untold meaning. Who was writing to her mother and making her feel weirded out? She sighed.

A voice interrupted her thoughts. 'Hey, Class Swot, you done the homework?' Turning her face from the steamed-up window, where she'd left a smudged imprint of her nose and forehead, Willow looked at the boy sitting next to her. The geeky black-rimmed glasses perched on his freckled nose gave him the air of a 1950s American cartoon character.

1

'Less of the swot, Java. Takes one to know one.' Willow smiled at her friend, Jarvis. His nickname was Java—a nod to the computer language JavaScript that he so lovingly banged on about.

'Can I read the homework?' Stella asked from behind. 'I love your stories.'

'Eww, won't you barf everywhere?' Jarvis winced.

'Why would I *barf* reading one of Willow's stories?' Stella asked.

'Because reading on the bus always makes *me* want to spew,' Jarvis replied, wrinkling up his nose dramatically.

'Oh, is this one of those twin things?' Willow asked eagerly. Jarvis looked puzzled. 'You know: if one of you is sick, the other one is too? Because you are twins. Supernatural weirdness stuff. *You know*!' Willow rolled her eyes.

Jarvis's twin, Stella, laughed and combed her immaculate blonde bob smooth with her fingers. 'Oh yes, I forgot we were twins! How silly of me. I didn't put on my matching coat and shoes today. Willow, quick, punch Jarvis in the face and see if I can feel it as well.'

Jarvis put up his hands to protect himself from the play punch Willow was about to deliver. 'Not the face, not the face!' So Willow walloped him in the arm instead, making him shout, 'Oi!'

Stella gripped her corresponding arm and groaned in an over-the-top manner. 'That really hurt, Willow. I bet I'm going to have to have it in a sling for the rest of the day and not be able to write. Quick, do it again!'

Willow shook her head, laughing.

'You have to let me read your story now to make up for it then.'

'I need help with something else first,' Willow said, deciding that she had to prise her worry out of her head before it got comfy in there for one more day.

'Sure,' Stella said. 'Fire away.'

'Mum's being weird.'

'So what's new? Your mum is *always* weird,' Jarvis said.

'No, I mean a new level of weird that outdoes all the other weirdness that usually goes on. She's getting letters that make her freak out.'

'Freak out how?' Stella asked.

'She just has to look at the envelope on the days I have given her the post and even if she has been laughing she goes white, grabs it, and then ignores me for the rest of the time until bed.'

'That doesn't sound good,' Jarvis said. 'Do you know who they're from?'

'Not a clue. She never opens them in front of me. But it's the same curly black handwriting every time.'

3

'Hmm,' Stella said in her best Sherlock Holmes voice raising one eyebrow at the same time, something Willow always wished she could do but just couldn't pull off. 'Have you tried asking her who they're from?'

'Yes, but she just fobbed me off saying they were for her to deal with. Someone wants her to do some work for them and she doesn't want to, and they won't leave her alone.'

'That sounds plausible,' Jarvis said.

'Yeah, but why would they write?' Stella wondered out loud. 'With all the technology in the world, you would have thought they would email, ring, text.'

'I know,' Willow replied despondently. 'But I sort of get it; Mum is such a technophobe. She can't work her phone most of the time, let alone check emails. So maybe snail mail is the last resort?'

'It sounds fairly dodgy to me,' Jarvis said. 'How often are they coming?'

'So far, I have noticed one a week for the last few weeks.'

'Have you looked at the postmark?' Jarvis asked. 'You know, to see where they're coming from.'

'No! Good idea! I wish I had. I can look next time, though it won't tell me who they're from.'

'Well, you know what you have to do then?' Jarvis said mysteriously.

'No, what?' Willow replied.

'Open one.'

'I couldn't do that. Mum would go mental. It would feel wrong going behind her back.'

'But she's not telling you the truth. Or you *think* she isn't,' Stella said.

Willow sighed. The twins were right. She needed to see what was in those letters. 'I need to do it without her finding out that I've looked.'

'Well, you are talking to the right man then,' and Jarvis winked.

'Java! What!?' Willow and Stella cried.

'Operation Steal a Letter!' Jarvis said, hushing them in case anyone could hear. Not that anyone was listening to the three thirteen-year-olds hatching their underhand plan. The bus was rammed with kids heading to school and the noise that a packed bus of kids generated drowned out any of the threesome's chit-chat. 'I have a sketchy idea in my head. Let's reconvene after morning break and I will have had time to solidify my ideas into a proper plan of action. All will be revealed then.'

Willow couldn't stop laughing at Jarvis's spy talk but let him get on with working out the plan in his head. She could almost hear his robotic brain ticking over as he sat next to her on the bus.

Meanwhile Stella was more interested in whom Willow thought the mysterious sender was. 'It's quite exciting really,' Stella mused from the seat behind. 'I mean, it could be anyone.'

'Like who . . . ?' Willow asked, sitting sideways so she could see Stella properly.

'Like your real mum. You know, your mad mum, Helen, isn't *really* your mum. She snatched you from a pram all those years ago and now a private detective has tracked you down and they are onto her. Maybe you are really related to the Royal Family or a Hollywood star?' Willow laughed.

'Or maybe she's not who she says she is? Maybe you and she are in the witness protection programme and the police want to move you to another village because the guy she put away in jail is about to be released into the public and they are scared for your safety . . . ?' Stella was off on a wild goose chase with possible letter writers. 'Or how about your mum has been asked to do the album cover of Lost and Found's rivals, One Man Standing? Could it be that? And they're trying to poach her, sending her money in the post!!'

'Hmm, we could do with some money at the mo,' Willow sighed. 'I'm getting a bit sick of beans on toast.' Life as an artist wasn't the best-paid job. It was a bit feast and famine in the Fitzpatrick household some months.

'Remember, guys, meet me at the oak tree bench at morning break. I will reveal my ingenious plan . . . '

Willow and Stella rolled their eyes as they grabbed their bags. 'Jarvis and his lame plans,' Stella said scathingly. 'I can't actually believe he would come up with anything *useful*.'

'Willow, would you stay behind after class?' Mrs Bannister asked at the end of their English lesson.

'Yes, Mrs Bannister.'

As the class roused themselves from the slumber of English and clattered and scraped back chairs, Willow wondered what her teacher could possibly want.

'What have you been up to?' Willow's friend, Sadie asked. 'Setting light to desks again?'

'Or maybe she's been writing swear words all over the walls of the girls' loos?' Stella joined in.

'I think it was when you smashed up the Year Thirteen common room,' Sadie replied, laughing. The thought of Willow doing any of those things was crazy. She was a good girl and trouble wasn't in her vocabulary.

Willow shrugged and slowly packed her books away in her super cool old-school orange satchel. One of the stray pencils on her desk made its way into her purposely messy topknot for safekeeping.

When the classroom was empty she walked to her teacher's desk.

'I'm looking forward to reading your homework,' Mrs Bannister said. 'Sit down, won't you?' Willow grabbed a nearby chair. 'Have you heard of *The Sunday Times* New Young Writers' Competition?' Willow shook her head. Mrs Bannister slid a photocopied newspaper page towards her on the desk. 'Take this home and have a read. I think we should enter you.'

'Oh, wow,' Willow breathed. 'Really?'

'Yes, really! It's for writers aged thirteen to sixteen, and then sixteen to nineteen, and so on. I think it would be good practice for you to try and write a long piece, a real project for you to get your teeth into.' Willow liked the sound of that. 'We have until the summer to get it in and it will be judged over the summer holidays. The winners are announced in the autumn. What do you think?'

Willow nodded. 'What do I have to write about?' They were in March now, so she had a while.

'Anything you like. It doesn't even have to be a story. It can be anything. But they give you suggestions and ideas in the copy I gave you.' Willow picked it up. 'I thought I would give you a book to inspire you.' And she handed Willow a beaten-up paperback.

'*Little Women*?' Willow asked. 'What's it about?'

'A family drama set in the American Civil War in the 1860s. I think it will appeal to you. Seeing as you always write so convincingly about family dramas.'

Willow blushed. She did manage to somehow shoehorn a family issue into any writing homework Mrs Bannister gave them . . .

'Thank you.'

'So what's the plan, Java?' Stella asked as soon as Willow joined them on the bench under the oak tree in the front of the school 'chill' area.

'When do you think there will be another letter landing on the doorstep?' he asked Willow, ignoring Stella's question.

'Er . . . ' Willow screwed her eyes up and had a think. 'I think either tomorrow or the day after. They are roughly a week apart.'

'Great. That means we can get on it as soon as possible!' Jarvis clapped his hands together and explained what he wanted Willow to do.

'But what if it isn't tomorrow?' Willow said worriedly when he had finished outlining his plan.

'The plan can be put on hold until it is. It will be OK.'

Chapter Two
Operation Steal a Letter

'You're going to be late,' Mum said, glancing yet again at the giant silver-rimmed clock on the kitchen wall. It was edging ever nearer to must-leave-the-house time. Willow was dawdling at breakfast, stretching out her Marmite and toast as long as she could. 'The twins will be here any second.' Mum didn't normally care about Willow being late for school!

'They're going to the dentist this morning, so aren't going to call.' Of course it was all a lie and part of Jarvis's grand plan: Operation Steal a Letter. The twins would be waiting at the bus stop. Mum would go out for her bike ride in the opposite direction and Willow would wait for the post like they'd planned. She would get the next bus, after the postman had been, and be ever so slightly late for school. Willow would go back to the twins' house after school where they would steam open the letter, read it, then reseal it with glue and get the twins to post it through the letterbox on the way to school the next day.

11

'But you have to go; you'll miss the bus.' Mum looked right at her, almost into her very brain where the deceptive plan was lurking, waiting to spring into action.

Willow gulped. Could her mum tell she was up to something? Willow had never been up to 'something' in her life! It was quite an alien concept for her to lie and pretend to Mum she wasn't trying to steal the post.

'I won't; I'll be fine. The twins always walk so slowly; I'll be quicker on my own. Aren't you going on your bike ride?' Willow asked casually. Her mum always went for a bike ride every morning to clear her head and get some exercise before she started working on her sculptures. Willow could always tell if she hadn't gone for one —it was as though she needed to go out of the house to find her brain every morning!

'I was going to have a coffee first to give me some energy and then go for a long bike ride after that.' Doh! It was a Mexican stand-off, neither of them moving. Any minute now Willow was going to have to leave because Mum hadn't even started making her coffee and she had a ritual when it came to making coffee: the warming of the cafetière with boiling water; heating the milk in the microwave. It took ages.

Willow suddenly had an idea to buy some time.

'Mum, I think we're almost out of coffee and a lot of the basics. I'm just going to check we've enough money for a mini shop.' She stood up and grabbed the iPad on charge by the kettle. She went straight to her folder and opened the spreadsheet of their incomings and outgoings that Stella had created so that Willow could keep track of their money and they could manage a budget.

'It looks as though we've got some cash left this week, so that's good.' Willow smiled at her mum, sitting back down with the iPad and pretending to look through her spreadsheet at anything pending. *Someone* had to be in charge and her mum could never remember what she had spent and what bills needed paying when. Willow was glad she hadn't inherited her mum's scatty nature.

'OK, peanut, I'll go later. But you should leave now or you really will miss the bus.'

Willow reluctantly started to put on her coat having thoughts of abandoning the whole plan; if she ran for the bus now she could just about make it. Suddenly there was the familiar sound of the letterbox flapping in the hallway behind them and the flop of letters landing on the Union Jack doormat.

'The post is *really* early!' Mum exclaimed loudly. 'Maybe it's loads of junk mail.' It *was* fairly early for the post to be dropped off, but not unheard of in their tiny village where there wasn't a huge amount of post to be delivered.

Willow was already up with her coat on. She swung her bag onto her shoulder and headed for the front door. 'I'll get it on my way out.' She could see from the kitchen door that a cream envelope was stacked in between some bills and a supermarket flyer. She had about ten seconds to steal the letter before Mum would find out. She had to be quick. Her bag was already open.

Please stay sitting down, Mum, Willow prayed as she bent down to pick up the post. She slipped the cream envelope into her bag as she was doubled over the doormat. Her hands were shaking. She didn't even know if it *was* one of the letters; she hadn't looked at the writing because it was facing the other way when she had grabbed it. Better to be safe than sorry, she thought.

Her mum had followed her out into the hallway, but, because it was so narrow, she had to wait by the kitchen door and hadn't seen Willow take the letter. Willow shoved the post at her and smiled. 'I'd better go; the bus will be here in a mo. Have a good day working!' And she bent forward and kissed her mum, who was already looking through the post, on the cheek.

'Bye, love. Have a good day. See you later.' Willow walked calmly down the driveway and on to Raker's

Lane. The minute she got past the old oak and out of sight, she started running like an escaped lunatic. Which was what she felt like. Past her Granna's house she ran, her hair trailing out behind her like a mermaid underwater. She could see the bus stop on the green and the bus pulling up. The twins spotted her haring over to them and waited until the last minute before getting on, making sure the bus didn't go without her.

The bus driver rolled his eyes and shut the doors behind them before they even had a chance to get a seat. Willow rummaged in her bag for her pass, flashed it at the driver, and then the three of them picked their way through the grannies and their shopping trolleys, and the older kids, to the very back of the bus.

'So?' Jarvis asked as he slumped into his seat. 'Did you get it?'

'I don't know.' And she told them about the stand-off and how she suspected Mum had been waiting for the post as well. But then again, she couldn't be sure.

'Let's see it then!' Stella gasped.

Willow opened her bag and groped around until she pulled it out like a rabbit from a hat. 'Ta da!' She turned the envelope over to look at the writing; it was the same as the writing on all the others. 'The postmark says SE London.'

'That must mean south-east London. I wish we could steam it open now,' Jarvis sighed. 'It's just too exciting!'

'I wonder what it's going to say?' Stella asked.

'We won't know until after school,' Jarvis said, rubbing his hands together. 'Can we bear the suspense?' They all shook their heads as Willow held the letter up to the window to see if she could see anything through the envelope. But the paper was so thick they'd need X-ray vision to even have a chance at a sneaky peek.

The school day dragged its heels, making all three of them check their watches every five minutes in every lesson. Willow could feel the letter pulsing with possibilities in her bag. She felt slightly nervous because, in a way, she didn't want to know what was inside it. And yet she did. And then again she didn't. Her mind was playing a pantomime game with her conscience.

The bell rang to signal the end of the day and all three of them practically pushed everyone else out of the way to get to the bus stop just outside the school gates. They scrambled for seats and sat in silence on the journey home. As the bus came to a halt at their stop, the kids jumped off and raced up the lane to Willow's house, round the side, down to Willow's mum's shed studio, and burst through the door.

'Hi, Mum. I'm just going next door; I'll be back in a bit.'

Her mum was working on the sculpture for the latest Lost and Found album cover. She was listening to loud rock music. The sculpture looked like one of those amazing Hindu altarpieces. But if you looked really closely, you could see it was made up of lots of teeny tiny bits of broken toys and odd bits of Lego, some of it painted gold and silver.

'Wow, Helen, it looks . . . amazing!' Jarvis said.

'Why, thank you, Jarvis. That's very kind. If you have any old bits of cars or anything you don't want, please do fling them my way. They will be put to good use. How was the dentist this morning?'

Mum had her back to them so Willow made a face that he should answer.

'Er, yes, it was fine. Just a check-up.'

The three of them bundled through the gate and into the house, giggling nervously. Hannah, the twins' older sister, was in; her car was in the drive. But their parents wouldn't be back till half past six.

'Cup of tea?' Jarvis winked.

'Don't mind if I do,' Stella replied. 'Willow?'

Willow nodded. Her stomach was churning now and her palms were sweaty; she rubbed them dry on her school skirt. As the kettle boiled, the moment of truth dawned upon them. They were really going to do this. Actually steam open the envelope. Jarvis took it from her and gingerly placed the sealed part fairly close to the steam, careful not to burn his fingers. All three of them were solemnly silent. The only sound was the kettle bubbling away into a frenzy before it stopped and the button clicked, turning it off. Jarvis placed the letter on the worktop and, with a butter knife, slowly eased the seal apart. When it was fully open he handed it to Willow.

'I believe the honour is all yours.'

Willow gulped. Was she ready for this? She pulled the letter from its protective sheath, unfolded it, and began to read . . .

Chapter Three
Anthony Jerrard

Willow couldn't decipher the writing at first. There was an address printed at the top in dark purple fancy text on very posh watermarked paper. That bit she read: *Anthony Jerrard, 136 Melbourne Grove, London SE22 8SA.* And an email address and mobile number. Willow shook her head and screwed her eyes and nose up. He had obviously written in a hurry. There was only one tiny paragraph to read.

Dear Helen

I told you I was going to write weekly until I heard from you. We need your help, please. Urgently. After this letter, I will write every day. I don't want this to lead to me having to camp outside your house just so we can talk.

Regards
Anthony

'What does it say?' both twins gasped. Willow handed them the letter.

'Ooh, spidery writing!' Jarvis exclaimed.

'What do you think it means?' Stella asked after reading it.

Willow shrugged. 'I don't know. Maybe it's work-related, like Mum said.' There really was nothing to go on.

'Well, he must really want her to work for him because he's willing to camp outside!' Stella said.

'We could Google him,' Jarvis suggested. 'Then we might know who he is.'

'Good idea!' Stella said and jumped up from the stool.

'What's the point?' Willow said. 'It really does look like a work thing. Mum was telling the truth. If I look him up, then I will know who he is, and know something about a letter I shouldn't have even stolen. What if I ever slip up and it comes out? Mum will know and I will be in trouble over something that's not even exciting.'

'How do you mean, slip up? "Oh, Mum, I accidentally stole a letter and know a man called Anthony is trying to force you to work for him." ' Stella laughed. 'Don't be daft, you can forget about it now. It's just work. But don't you want to see who he is, just in case it *could* be something else? What if you bump into him waiting outside? At least you will know who he is and what he does. Your mum could be a spy, and the art is all a front, and this man Anthony is her boss, asking her to do one last undercover job!'

Willow laughed. 'You know, Stella, sometimes I think it's you with the writing talent because you think up such crazy stuff all the time.'

Willow was torn. She did want to peek, but she didn't at the same time. Pantomime mind games again. The twins were looking at her intently.

'He may not even be anyone. He might not be on there,' Jarvis cooed.

'OK, let's look then. But just quickly 'cos I told Mum I would be back in a bit.'

All three ran up the floating staircase. Well, not quite. Willow's fear of falling through the steps checked her desire to get to the computer quickly.

Jarvis flipped open the laptop on Stella's desk and switched it on. Immediately, the computer began to install some software updates. 'Why do they always do that when you're in a rush?' Willow complained.

'Artificial intelligence, see? It does exist. The

computer is trying to wind you up!' Jarvis smirked. After a few moments, Jarvis got onto the internet. 'How do you spell his surname?' he asked Willow. She told him.

'Wow,' breathed Stella as a whole stream of sites snaked down the screen, all claiming to hold information about Anthony Jerrard.

'Which one?' Willow asked. As she skim-read them, she worked out he was a writer.

'This one,' Jarvis said confidently and clicked on a site that looked like the official Anthony Jerrard website. Up popped a picture of a man in his forties, a good-looking surfer type with long swept-back salt-and-pepper hair. 'Ooh, he's a bit of a dude. He looks really familiar!'

'Yes, I've seen him before,' Stella agreed. 'Maybe on the telly?' Jarvis suddenly jumped up and ran downstairs, taking them two at a time. Willow winced, waiting for the crash and the trip to A and E as he fell through the gaps.

Willow started reading the blurb on the home page.

Anthony Jerrard has been a successful journalist for twenty years. His 'Man About Town' column in the *Guardian* is

observational writing at its best and has
won many awards over the years. He has
recently branched out into writing books.
His first novel *My Life in Smells*, a
fictional memoir about a lost childhood,
was published last year to rave reviews
and has already been shortlisted for two
literary prizes.

Click *here* for an extract.

Willow scanned the rest of the page listing the awards and found what she was looking for at the bottom.

Anthony likes relaxing at home in south-
east London with his wife, cookery writer
Maria McVey, and their two children.

It was definitely him if it said south-east London, just like the postmark! Just then Jarvis crashed back into the room.

'Look!' he shouted. 'I found this downstairs. I *knew* I'd seen him before!' And he brandished a hardbacked book, *My Life in Smells*. 'I saw Dad reading it recently.'

'It's him!' Willow breathed. She took the book from

Jarvis and turned to the back cover flap. The author stared back at her, the same picture as on the website.

'I wonder what he wants Mum to do for him?'

'Maybe he really wants her to make something for his next book cover, like she does for Lost and Found, and he's just going to keep hassling her until she gives in?' Stella suggested.

'Yes, it's probably something like that,' Willow agreed. 'Oh, I hope she does it. It would be so exciting for her to do something book-related. And maybe I could get to meet him. I should read his book first, of course.'

'You can't! What if your mum finds it in the house? She'll know you stole the letter.'

'Yeah, good point. Well, I don't have to read it yet; she's not even agreed to do the cover yet. We need to put the letter back in the envelope and seal it all up. So you'll drop it in the letterbox tomorrow after we've left for school?' Stella nodded.

'See you later, guys,' Willow said the next day as she and the twins parted ways on the lane in front of their houses. School was over and it was Friday, Willow's favourite day of the week. And, even better than that, it was the start of the Easter holidays. Willow was feeling great.

'Is your mum making fajitas for dinner tonight?' Stella asked hopefully.

'Yeah, Stella. Don't worry, I'm sure she hasn't forgotten it's movie night!' Willow replied as she walked up the drive. That evening Stella was due round to Willow's house for tea. Most Fridays Mum would cook fajitas and all three of them would sit down and watch a cheesy film in the living room in front of the fire (even in the summer if Stella begged!); something she loved as she had nothing like that in her ultra modern, open-plan home with no nooks or crannies. Sometimes Jarvis would come if he wasn't mending iPhones or hooking up with one of his spoddy mates.

'Enjoy your saddo romcom,' Jarvis laughed sarcastically over his shoulder.

'You're just jealous,' Stella shot back.

'Hardly! I wouldn't be caught dead watching that rubbish.'

'Children! Stop fighting,' Willow joked, wondering for the millionth time what it would be like to have an annoying brother to bicker with. She often felt as though something was missing from her very small family of two . . . well, three if you included Granna.

As Willow opened the front door, she could hear

voices coming down the short corridor from the kitchen. It sounded like Mum was talking to Granna.

'She's here,' she heard Granna say. 'Is that you, pet?'

Willow walked into the kitchen, dumping her satchel on the floor by the doorway. Mum and Granna were sitting at the kitchen table, drinking coffee. Mum was facing Willow with Granna on her left.

'Hi!' Mum said. Something was wrong. They both looked very, very serious, and Mum looked as though she had been crying.

'What's going on?' Willow asked with a sinking feeling in her tummy.

'Come and sit down, pet,' Granna said quietly.

'No, not until you tell me what's going on,' Willow challenged them.

'May as well cut to the chase, Helen,' Granna said, sighing.

'Willow, I don't really know how to start this conversation,' Mum said, sounding drained of all energy. She looked for support at Granna, who nodded at her to carry on.

'You know I have always told you your father was a sperm donor?' Willow nodded, her heart suddenly pounding in her ears. Her tongue suddenly felt too big for her mouth and her throat was dry.

'Well, he isn't.'

'He isn't a sperm donor?'

'No, he was an old boyfriend.'

'What does that mean? That he donated sperm because you wanted a baby?' Willow was referring to the story Mum had told her about her birth. That was what Willow had always understood to be the truth. Her mum had wanted a baby so, rather than wait for Mr Right, she had used a sperm donor.

'Not exactly . . . '

'Just tell her, pet,' Granna said softly.

Mum cleared her throat. 'I was with this guy for years; we met in the last year of uni and then stayed together for eight years. We drifted apart towards the end and, just as we split up, I found out I was pregnant with you.'

Willow looked at Granna as her mum stopped to take a sip of coffee.

'I didn't know what to do. I was single, your dad had already met someone else—the woman he is now married to—and I had a career that still hadn't taken off.'

'What did you do?' Willow whispered as she finally sat down, then shook her head, realizing that Mum had gone ahead and had her.

'I went to counselling to help me decide. They gave

me a scan, and there on the screen was a tiny baby with a heartbeat. I was over three months pregnant. I'd no idea I was that far into the pregnancy.'

'But what about my dad?' Her mum stayed quiet. 'Mum?' Willow asked in a shaky voice.

'He agreed to pay for you for the rest of your life.'

'That's *it*? Does he know anything about me?' Her mum shook her head.

'Then why are you telling me any of this? I don't understand. He doesn't want to know about me, doesn't know who I am, so why tell *me* about *him*?'

'Because he was going to turn up at the house. I had to tell you before he arrived.'

'What's his name?' Willow asked, starting to feel queasy. A penny had dropped somewhere in her head.

'Anthony.' Willow thought she was going to pass out.

'Anthony *Jerrard*?' she screeched.

'Yes! How did you know that?'

'Because I worked it out!' Willow was at full volume now.

'How? How did you work it out, exactly?' Mum started to sound slightly hysterical.

'He's the man sending the letters.'

'How do you know that?' Helen shot back like machine-gun fire.

28

'Because I opened one!' Willow shouted, her voice cracking from the effort of being so loud.

'You did *what*?'

'Helen! Calm down! I told you something like this was going to happen one day.' Granna placed her hand on her daughter's clenched fist and patted her.

Willow stayed silent. She wanted to scream at her mum, but her throat was now hurting from shouting. How dare she tell her off for peeking when she had been lying for all these years?

'Why is he writing letters?' Willow asked, steadying her voice to keep the anger in check. *Her* father was a famous writer. It was almost totally unbelievable. Willow was expecting the twins to pop up in the middle of the kitchen and shout 'April Fool!', but it was too early. So this must be real. Anthony Jerrard is my dad, Willow thought, waiting for her mum to give the answer that would change her life forever . . .

Chapter Four
Instant family

Willow held her breath. She watched her mum as she screwed her face up as though she was anticipating a punch.

'Because his daughter is very sick. The daughter he had with his wife after we split up. He has a son too.' She had a sister? And a brother! Willow's head was spinning.

'You *knew* I had a brother and a sister. I can't believe this!' Willow bellowed, not caring if she hurt her throat this time. 'You always told me it was how it was meant to be just me. But you *knew* all along.'

Mum bowed her head, as though she didn't know what to say.

'Let your mum finish what she has to say, pet,' Granna said gently. 'I know you're so angry, it's understandable, but there's more to this. Your sister is ill.'

'What's wrong with her?' Willow snapped, slightly calmer.

'She has a disease called aplastic anaemia,' Mum continued. 'It means her bone marrow doesn't work and, unless she has a bone marrow transplant, she won't recover.'

'So why does that mean he's hassling you? How can *you* help?'

Mum took a deep breath. 'It's not me that can help, Willow. It's you.'

'How?' Willow couldn't even begin to imagine how she could help her dying sister she didn't know about until less than a minute ago.

'Anthony wants you to be tested as a bone marrow match for Bella, his daughter. There isn't a matching donor on any registry anywhere. No one in his immediate family is a match.'

Willow was stunned.

'Willow, pet, shall I make you a cup of tea?' Willow nodded automatically.

Mum leaned over the table and grabbed Willow's hand, but Willow snatched it away and looked at her mum, stony-faced. She felt numb—as though she needed to smash her head against a wall to feel something. Willow didn't lose her temper very often but this had shocked her to her very core. Everything she had thought was real was fake.

'How could you lie?' she hissed at her mum. 'How *could* you? After all the chat you gave me about both of us being honest and always telling the truth. As long as we tell the truth we will always be OK, you said.'

Granna placed the cup of tea in front of Willow. Her hand was shaking and a tiny bit of tea slopped over the edge and onto the table. Willow absently rubbed it away with her hand.

'If you don't mind, I would like to say something, since I am as guilty as anyone in this situation, in terms of not telling you the truth about your father,' Granna said.

'Go ahead,' Mum said, visibly relieved that she didn't have to answer her daughter's difficult question.

'When Helen got pregnant it was no doubt a big decision to be a single mother, and not one she took lightly. Anthony never said she shouldn't have the baby—he was never not going to support your mum; he just wanted to do it secretly. He had just started a new life with his now wife—I can't remember her name . . . '

'Maria,' Helen interjected.

'Yes, with Maria. He thought that having a baby with someone he wasn't even with any more would ruin his chances with her. This is what he told us, anyway.'

'So it wasn't that he didn't want kids; he just didn't

want . . . me.' Willow could feel tears pricking behind her eyes. Her anger had been extinguished and instead she felt overwhelmed with sadness. Her dad didn't want her . . .

'No!' her mum almost shouted. 'That's the thing, Willow. This story is so long and complicated that it twists and turns more times than a cobra. He *did* want you. He wanted a baby with me before we were even thirty. He was ready to settle down, get married, have kids—all the traditional stuff that I run away from. That's why we split up, because I didn't want any of those things.'

'But you had me! Why couldn't you stay together when you knew I was there?'

'Because he had already left. We had broken up. He was in love with Maria. The timing was all wrong. I was having his baby two years too late and he had moved on. You see, he did want you; it was *me* he didn't want. As mad as it sounds now, we decided that if he was to be happy and I was to be happy, no contact would take place.'

'But what about what *I* wanted?' Willow started crying properly now, tears running unchecked down her cheeks. Her mum got up to come and sit next to Willow and put her arms around her shoulders but Willow just shrugged her off. She didn't want to be touched. Her mum remained quiet.

'Does he even know what I look like?'

'I sent him one picture when you were born,' Granna said. 'And we never heard anything from him after that, just monthly payments into my bank account which I gave to your mum in cash, so you wouldn't know about them in years to come. And as his wages went up, so did the payments. Those payments are what keep you and your mum afloat in lean times when she's between art projects.'

'Do you ever contact him?' Willow asked, rubbing her eyes furiously to try to stem the tears.

'I did write to him to tell him we were moving out of Granna's when I bought this cottage, but never heard back, until now. But it's better this way. You get to live with me all the time. No having to go to London on the train every other weekend. We get to have an uninterrupted life here and live in peace. He supports you and you have a happy life here in the country.'

'Yes, but what about when he asked about Bella? What did you do?'

Mum turned her eyes shamefully to the tabletop and examined an imaginary crumb. 'I ignored him at first. He kept writing and wouldn't leave it. After that letter this morning, the one I gather you already opened, I rang him on his mobile and told him you wouldn't be helping, and to leave us alone. I looked up the operation on the internet and I didn't want you to have to go through that. Especially knowing how you hate anything to do with blood and needles.'

'Mum! What did he say?' Willow screeched, her anger flaring up again and drying her remaining tears in an instant.

'He threatened to come up at the weekend and sit outside the house until I agreed to talk to him. I didn't want him telling you anything. So Granna and I thought it best to tell you. Granna thinks it's your choice, not mine.' Granna nodded her head sagely.

Willow looked at both of them, shaking her head in disbelief. 'So I'm supposed to just make up my mind, here? Right now?'

'No, I—' Helen started to talk but Willow wouldn't let her.

'I don't get it. You both kept this from me my whole life and now I'm supposed to just be like, "Oh, hi Dad. Great to finally meet you. Yes, of course I will have a blood test and help rescue your *real* daughter." ' Willow stood up so hastily, her chair smashed backwards onto the kitchen floor. 'You have got to be kidding me . . .'

'Please don't,' Helen said. 'We need to talk some more. You might have more questions.'

'I need to see Stella.' And Willow got up, strode across the kitchen to the door, and was gone.

Chapter Five
The Not Meant To Be Here Club

'Crikey, Willow! You scared me!' said Hannah, looking shaken. Willow had run across the lawn and banged on the sliding door to be let in next door. 'Are you OK? You look white as a sheet.'

'I'm fine,' she lied. Willow didn't want to talk to anyone except Stella. 'Can I go up?'

'Be my guest.'

Willow for once forgot her fear of the dreaded stairs and took them two at a time. She crashed into Stella's room.

'Willow? What's happened?' asked Stella. It was blindingly obvious that Willow was in a bit of a state. Bursting into a room was something Willow never did.

Willow just stood there, staring at her. Now she felt stupid for being dramatic and sat down on the bed and just said what was on her mind: 'Anthony Jerrard is my dad.'

'Exsqueeze me?!' Jarvis said in a mock computerized voice, listening in from the doorway behind them both. 'Does not compute. Please repeat what you just said.'

'Java, out!' Stella said sternly. 'This is important and you're not invited.'

Jarvis looked as though he was going to start a massive counter-attack and then thought better of it.

'No, it's OK, Stella. I need him to hear this too.' Jarvis gave Stella a superior smile and stepped into the room and leaned against the wall.

Willow sighed and looked at them both in turn. 'Anthony Jerrard, the man writing the letters, is my dad.'

'No way!' Stella shouted. 'I knew there was something weird going on with those letters!'

'Oh, it gets better,' Willow said and relayed the whole story, or as much as she could remember. Not all of it had gone in.

The twins listened, transfixed, until she had finished, gawping at her with open mouths.

'No wonder you're so good at writing,' Stella breathed excitedly. 'Your dad is a famous writer! Wow . . . '

'But I feel so cross!' Willow exploded. 'They all lied for years. Anthony isn't my proper dad. He just wants to know me now because I might be able to help Bella.'

'Well, yes,' Stella agreed. 'It does seem pretty rubbish when you look at it like that.'

'What about your mum?' Jarvis asked. 'Are you cross with her or just with your dad?'

'With all of them, Granna too. How could they do that to me?'

All three sat there, looking puzzled. Willow was so confused – why did grown-ups have to mess things up?

'I guess, in the end, your mum was just doing what she thought best for both of you,' Stella said eventually.

'Yes. If Bella had never got sick, you would never have found out anything and lived happily ever after,' Jarvis agreed.

Willow nodded, realizing that maybe Mum had been in a hard position at the time. If Anthony hadn't wanted to be with her, and Mum had wanted to keep the baby, what choice did she have? It still didn't make it OK, though.

'You're lucky, really,' Jarvis said. 'It could have been like it was with Hattie's parents and got nasty. At least you have always been without a dad, and at least he paid your mum. Imagine being Hattie?'

At the end of last year, Hattie, a girl in their year, hadn't come in to school one day. When she appeared a week later she was beside herself. No one knew what had happened to her. It turned out her dad had run off with a family friend, taken all the money from the joint account, taken the car, filed for divorce, and disappeared. Hattie, her brother, and little sister hadn't seen him since. Hattie had been heartbroken. It had been top scandal until February when something else happened to knock it off the top spot.

'At least Anthony didn't have a . . . what was it Hattie's dad had? That thing her mum said it was? What was it?' Jarvis continued.

'Midlife crisis,' Willow remembered. 'He was having one of those. Grown-ups have them when they think they are too old. Or something like that.' Willow did not get grown-ups sometimes.

'So really you are very lucky to be welcomed into a new club,' Jarvis said opening his arms wide and gesticulating madly.

'And what club would that be?' Stella asked, rolling her eyes.

'The Not Meant To Be Here Club! You're an accident, just like me and Stella!'

Willow laughed for the first time that afternoon.

'We can have club meetings now and discuss what it's like to be here by accident, and how that shapes us as human beings.'

Stella threw a pillow at Jarvis's head. 'Speak for yourself. I'm definitely supposed to be here!'

'So what are you going to do?' Jarvis asked, dodging the pillow.

'I dunno. The thing is, I don't even know anything about the disease Bella has.'

'Can you remember what it was called so I can Google it?' Stella said, sitting down next to the laptop.

Willow thought hard. She didn't know if it was leukaemia—that was the disease she had heard of where you might need a bone marrow transplant. 'If I heard it I would know what it is. Can you ask what sort of disease would need a bone marrow transplant?' Stella nodded.

A few sites came up and Stella clicked on them. She listed all the different types of leukaemia. Willow had no idea there were so many, but nothing rang a bell.

'Text your mum and ask,' Jarvis suggested.

'I left my phone at home.'

'How about this one, aplastic anaemia?' Stella said.

'Yes! That's it. Let me see.' Willow jumped over to Stella and started reading. "Aplastic anaemia is when the bone marrow fails to make blood cells and you have no blood count."

'What, you have no blood at all?' Jarvis cried. 'Like a robot?' And he started doing a robotic dance just to illustrate the point.

'No! You have no red blood cells,' Willow said as she read down the page. 'Meaning she would be bruised, tired, faint. She would need a bone marrow transplant from a matching donor, it says here. Eww!'

'What?' Jarvis and Stella said in unison.

'I can't read out what it says about the bone marrow operation. It's gross! And it talks about needles.' Both Jarvis and Stella read down the page, screwing up their noses.

If Willow was a match, she would have to have a general anaesthetic. She would lie face down on the bed and have needles inserted into her pelvis in her back. The needles would suck out her bone marrow from her pelvic bones. When the operation was over Willow would wake up and be able to go home the next day.

'That's a proper operation!' Jarvis exclaimed.

'Could you do that?' Stella asked tentatively. 'Your dad is asking a lot, isn't he? No wonder your mum was stressing every time she got a letter.'

'Yes, I know. But she still should have told me. It wouldn't be such a mess if she'd told me the truth. How can you not tell someone they have a family they've never met when you know it would be something they would love? I would feel so guilty all the time.'

'How do you know she isn't feeling guilty?' Stella suggested. 'She might have been ready to confess every time you said you wished you had a sister or weren't an only child. You won't know until you talk to her.'

'I'm not ready yet. I still feel like I could start smashing things even just thinking about it.'

'Whoa! Steady there!' Jarvis said. 'I don't fancy a black eye and I'm not sure Stella wants a trashed bedroom.'

'Don't worry, I'm not about to start smashing anything right now. Maybe later . . . ' Willow felt a lot calmer than she had done earlier. 'Let's look at Anthony again. I want to know more about him.'

Stella found his site straight away. It didn't give much away. 'Wow, now you look at that picture, you really do look like him, Willow,' Jarvis said, surprised.

'Maybe that's why you thought you had seen him before, Java,' said Stella. 'Because you had, every time you looked at Willow!'

'Put a long brown wig on him with pencils sticking out and you could be sisters! Well, mother and daughter . . . '

Willow stared at the screen, looking at the picture of the man who was her father. And, yes, there was a resemblance. An identical nose, eyes the same shape and colour, and the mouth was exactly like her own..

'How come we didn't notice before?' Stella wondered.

'Because we weren't looking,' replied Jarvis. 'It's like one of those creepy pictures you get on Facebook, where you have to spot the devil hiding in the sofa cushions. Takes you ages to see it if you *are* looking, so if you aren't looking, you'll never see it.'

'True,' Willow agreed.

'Let's see what else we can find out,' Stella said. She went back to her original search and scrolled down.

'Here we go. Look at this.' She had found an arts and entertainment site and there was an article about Anthony and his wife, Maria McVey. 'It says here that they were at some book awards ceremony in London and she won best new cookery writer or something. She's pretty, isn't she?'

'I don't want to look any more—it's weird,' Willow said, standing up. 'I think I'd better go back. Mum will think I'm planning to leave home or something. I know how her mind works.'

'OK. Do you know what you're going to do about it all?' Stella asked.

'No. Haven't a clue. I need to think about it but I can't because I don't want to think about it.' Willow's lip started wobbling again and she blinked away any rogue tears that threatened to fall. She hated crying and so far she had cried more in an hour than she had in the last three years.

'Then don't think about it,' Stella soothed, and stood up and gave her a massive hug, making Willow wilt and cry into her shoulder, finally letting someone comfort her properly.

'Don't forget, we're here if you need us,' Jarvis said awkwardly and came over and patted her back.

The movie night and fajitas were definitely off the menu now. Willow just wanted to stay in Stella's room for ever and never have to leave, but reality beckoned. Reality that felt like a crazy docudrama in which people cried every five minutes over a broken nail or streaky fake tan. Or suddenly finding out they had a dying sister who needed their bone marrow. . .

Chapter Six
Willow loses it

When Willow got home Granna had gone. Mum was sitting alone at the kitchen table with a glass of red wine and the bottle half empty next to it. Willow sat down opposite her mum and looked at her. She felt numb. A few hours ago her life was normal, even a bit boring, apart from the writing competition. She had no idea what to say to her mum. Thanks for ruining my life, perhaps?

'I'm so sorry,' Mum said in a small voice. 'I know you can't forgive me just yet, but I had no idea, really, what I was doing. I had never had a child before. I didn't know any of this would happen. I naively thought it would all work out for the best, just you and I together.'

Willow remained silent. She wanted to say it was OK, but it wasn't OK. None of it was. She could tell her mum hadn't done any of this to hurt her, but it was still the biggest shock in the world. What she really wanted to do was go to bed and lose herself in that new book

Mrs Bannister had lent her. Reading always helped her chill when she was feeling wrung out.

'What did Anthony say?'

'He doesn't know I've told you. I was waiting to see how it went.'

'How do you think it went?'

'As expected . . . ' Mum was wringing her hands and looked totally exhausted.

'And in the middle of all this Anthony wants me to make up my mind about a massive operation by when, Mum?' Willow could feel her anger building up again.

'I think he'll want an answer pretty much straight away.'

'How? How am I supposed to decide what to do? I don't even know him. Or her.'

'He wants to meet you.'

'But not because he *wants* to meet me. It's all wrong!'

'I know. I don't know what to do to make it better.'

'You should just have never lied!' Willow raged all over again. 'You should have told Anthony you were having his baby and that you would never lie to me about who my father was, so that one day I could turn up on his doorstep and shame him for leaving me!' Willow was shaking, the anger almost bursting out of the top of her head like a firework.

Her mum looked shocked. 'Yes, Willow. I know I shouldn't have lied. Hindsight is a terrible thing . . . '

'Not as terrible as finding out the two people who should love you the most in the world are massive liars, thought they could get away with it, and then make out they didn't have a choice.'

Mum's eyes filled with tears. She was speechless.

'Did you really think I would never find out I had a dad?' Willow shouted. If it had been a cartoon, her mum's hair would have been flying out behind her from the force of Willow's voice.

Mum shook her head, then nodded as though she was confused.

'It's like I never figured in any of this!'

'I know it looks like that, but I was thinking of you and how it would be easier in the end.'

'No, you weren't, you and Anthony were just thinking of yourselves. I'm going to bed. I'm not hungry anyway. I'll see you in the morning.' Willow stood up abruptly and pushed back her chair, scraping the floor with the chair legs.

'I understand, Willow,' Mum said sadly. But Willow ran up the stairs to her bedroom and slammed the door, not wanting to hear any more. She lay on her bed and stared out of the window into the still light sky, her tummy fizzing and a heavy feeling resting on her chest. She couldn't get over how Anthony thought he could waltz back into her life and say 'Hi, I'm your real dad. Now would you mind just donating your bone marrow? Thanks very much.' She wanted to throw something to find some sort of release. So one by one she grabbed the pretty floral scatter cushions from the head of her white metal-framed bed and chucked them at the shelves lining the opposite wall. She managed to hit a few paperbacks and they went flying dejectedly onto the fluffy white rug below.

That wasn't good enough. She really did need to smash something, to be destructive. She leaned up on her elbows and spotted an empty mug next to the bed—it must have been from tea in the morning. She picked it up and threw it at the wall opposite with such force it shattered everywhere, causing a rainfall of cold tea to splatter down the shelves and onto the now not so white rug below. The mug hadn't been empty.

Willow groaned at the mess and felt bad because she never did things like this, ever. But then she remembered why she had done it. Mum owed her at least a year of bad behaviour for this. She could probably carry out a carjacking without getting grounded this week.

She lay back on her pillows feeling spent, her anger having flown away with the mug. She knew at some point she would have to clear up the tea explosion. She stared at the ceiling, her eyes aching in their sockets. She closed them and let tears fall down into her ears, down her neck, and onto the pillow underneath. She felt as though she was a tap, and as the tears flooded out, her breathing slowed down until she was a bit calmer. When at last the tears stopped she reached for *Little Women* on her bedside table. So far she hadn't had a chance to read it, but now felt like the right time; she needed the distraction.

Contemplating the faded dog-eared cover of the book, Willow tried to register that she had a real live dad who wasn't a sperm donor. And he was an actual writer, just like Willow wanted to be. And in Real-Life Magazine Land he was some sort of celebrity. Her brain was just so rammed with all this new emotion-curdling information that thinking about Bella was unthinkable. Right then, the last thing she could ever contemplate was the dreaded blood test and, if she was a match, a possible operation with hideous needles. She was scared of it and didn't want to have to decide. The last time she had come face to face with a needle was her tetanus booster last term. The needle had been gargantuan and, as soon as she had seen it, she started feeling dizzy and sick. So when the nurse had jabbed it in her arm she had collapsed on the floor, hitting her head on the edge of a table, and ending up overnight in hospital with suspected concussion, proving to her that needles were evil. So the icing on the cake stuffed with surprise new family members and years of deceit was the fact she might have to face her dreaded fears.

Willow shook her head and turned the cover of the book to Chapter One. If she could escape for half an hour and sink into the story, she knew she would stop feeling so overwhelmed.

Willow started reading and, before she knew it, had been sucked into the world of Jo, Beth, Meg, and Amy March living in Orchard House during the American Civil War. As she turned the pages, she felt the story unfold in her heart. The Hello Kitty bedside clock on her rickety hand-painted cabinet said it was three o'clock in the morning by the time she ground to a halt and closed the book. Jo had just been sitting by Beth's bedside while she struggled to fight the scarlet fever which would almost kill her. Jo, the writer of the family and Beth's favourite sister, sat beside her throughout, mopping her brow and willing her to pull through. She did, just. Willow felt emotional and weepy reading it and knew she had to put it down before she was a sobbing heap again.

'I'd better get some sleep,' Willow said out loud to the room as if waiting for one of her books to suddenly agree with her from the shelves opposite. *Little Women* had taken her out of her world and into another one filled with sisters and adventures and family. Even though she loved them, books like these usually made Willow feel alone, but how could she feel alone that night, knowing that out there, somewhere, was a brand-new secret family just waiting to meet her? One thing was for sure: nothing was ever going to be the same again . . .

Chapter Seven
The morning after

Willow woke with a jump. She was still wearing her school uniform and her hair was all sweaty and matted. 'Why am I not in my PJs?' she mumbled to herself. Suddenly the previous day's events hit her. 'Oof,' she said, as if she had been punched in the stomach. Willow covered her eyes, trying to block out what had happened. She lay there reliving everything and groaning to herself. She squinted through her hands at the tea-splashed shelves Yes, she really had had a tantrum!

Despite her obvious trauma, her stomach started gurgling from lack of food. Willow could hear noises downstairs. It sounded like the crashing of pans. Was her mum cooking? She got up out of bed and opened the bedroom door. Yummy pancake-like smells wafted in. Willow hesitated. She didn't know what to say to her mum; she definitely wasn't ready to forgive her for all the lies. She had never had a massive falling out with her before so had no idea what it entailed, apart from feeling as though she needed to run away. Her stomach twisted and she almost retreated back into the safety of her room, but the lure of the pancakes was too strong to resist.

Willow pushed open the kitchen door. It wasn't pancakes; Mum was cooking Willow's favourite breakfast: French toast with maple syrup and chopped banana. It usually appeared amid clouds of smoke, setting off the familiar smoke alarm, but today it looked as though Mum was in the real world, concentrating on getting everything just right.

'You do know there's no school, don't you?' Mum said, pointing a fish slice at her, indicating her crumpled uniform.

'What? Oh yeah, I slept in it.'

'Would you like some breakfast?'

'Yes, please.' Willow could tell this breakfast was a plan to win her round. Mum dished it all up on a big plate with the bananas chopped just so in equal slices spread in a fan around the pieces of French toast.

'Thanks,' Willow said quietly and attacked the food hungrily. When she had stopped inhaling the French toast, her mum came and sat opposite her, nursing a mega mug of steaming coffee.

'So . . . ' she said as Willow finished up the last

few bits. 'How do you feel this morning?' She looked as though she didn't want to know the answer, almost flinching in anticipation of the reply.

Willow shrugged and stared at her plate. She felt all out of words, and for her that was unheard of. Willow had words for everything.

They sat there in silence for a few minutes while Willow chased a lone piece of banana round the plate with her fork until Mum spoke.

'Willow, I wish with all my might that I had done things differently. You're right, I should never have lied. Even if Anthony had wanted out, I still should have told you who he was.'

Willow sat motionless while her mum talked.

'But I can't change the fact that I did lie, so I don't know how I can make this better for you. All I can do is say you are the most important thing in my life; you always have been. There never was any question after I saw your heartbeat on that screen that I wasn't going to love you forever. And seeing you like this, so angry and sad, breaks my heart and it's all my fault. I wish I could take it away.'

Willow looked her mum in the eyes for the first time that morning. She knew her mum was telling the truth now. She half wanted to say it was all right; it didn't matter! But somehow the words wouldn't come out; she just wasn't ready to let it all be forgotten. This was too big a deal to sweep under the carpet. How could she forgive yet? She hadn't even met her dad. He might be a total idiot, Willow thought. That would be awful—worse than no dad at all!

'It's not *just* your fault, Mum. Anthony is part of it too. And Granna.' That was as close to 'I forgive you' that her mum was going to get today.

'Oh, Willow.' Mum reached over the table to show she'd got the message. She grabbed both Willow's hands in hers and this time Willow didn't try and snatch them away. Helen smiled and a single tear dropped onto her cheek. Willow wiped it away with her thumb.

'So is Anthony going to turn up today?' Willow asked uncertainly with a churning sensation deep in her belly. In all of this, she couldn't forget the reason for this mess—her sick half-sister. None of this was Bella's fault either . . .

'No chance!' her mum said, pulling herself together and standing up, gathering Willow's plate and cutlery. 'I told him I had told you and that you were in deep shock about having a father, let alone a brother and sister. And that as for his request, you had no answer.'

'What did he say?'

'He said thank you for listening, and sorry he had to force the issue. But he reminded me they didn't have lots of time.' She paused, as though she was thinking how best to phrase it all. 'But I don't want you rushing into anything, Willow. You have a proper think. This isn't just about helping Bella; this is about the rest of your life.'

Willow sat and thought for a moment. Something clicked in her head. 'Mum, what website did you look on when you looked up the bone marrow operation?'

'Oh, I can't remember. I think it was just the first one that came up. It was a cancer site—Macmillan or something like that.'

'Do you think it would be really scary? You know, going to hospital and everything?'

'I don't know, Willow. I've only ever been to hospital twice. Once to have you, and the other month when you smashed your head on the table at school and had to stay in overnight. I think this would be a bit different. Anyway, you haven't decided if you're going to be tested yet. And you may not even be a match for Bella, so you may not even have to go through it all.'

'I know. But what if I'm not a match—what happens then?'

'Well, hopefully they'll find someone on the donor registry eventually.'

'No, I mean, what happens to me?'

'With you and Anthony?' Willow nodded. 'I haven't got as far as that in my head yet,' her mum answered. 'This is why I was ignoring him, hoping he would go away, give up, and find someone else.'

'Why didn't he go away and find someone else?'

'Because the doctors told him there was a slight chance you could be a match and since then he has sort of ploughed on with the idea; obviously, he is pretty desperate.'

'But I know who he is now.' The question of 'what next?' hung unanswered between them in the air.

'Yes, you know who he is.' Her mum looked uncomfortable. 'I really am so sorry from the bottom of my heart, Willow. I really am. None of this was ever meant to hurt you; you must know that.'

'I know, Mum,' she said quietly. Willow wondered how long it would take to feel normal again with her mum. She hated being out of sorts like this. 'What's my . . . brother's name?'

'Archie. I think he's a few years younger than Bella.' Willow nodded. It still wasn't sinking in that she had a brother too.

'If you want to ask me anything else, anything at all, please do.'

Right now, thoughts were whizzing like racing cars round her head and she didn't have the energy to give this crazy situation in her life her full attention. All she wanted to do was check out of it for a few hours and come back to it later, when hopefully her brain would engage.

'Mum, I'm going to finish the book Mrs Bannister gave me, then I'll be down. Can we go for a bike ride after that?'

'Of course, peanut. Do what you have to do.'

So back upstairs Willow delved once more into the comforting world of the March sisters. Maybe they would help her make a decision.

Chapter Eight
The first step

'Mum, I think I should meet Anthony.' Willow stood in the doorway of the kitchen the following morning. She was quivering slightly and could feel her heart beating doubly fast in her ribcage.

Her mum looked up from her bowl of cereal, spoon mid-air on its way to her mouth, which remained open in a comic goldfish pose, while milk dripped all over the place. After the initial shock of Willow's statement, Mum seemed to recover. 'Wow! How did you come to a decision so quickly?'

Willow shrugged. She didn't want to reveal that she had always wondered who her dad was; she didn't want to hurt her mum's feelings, even though her mum had lied to her. Finishing *Little Women* had made her see that she had an opportunity to find out what it might be like to be in a bigger family, and Stella had persuaded her yesterday afternoon after the bike ride. 'Imagine the years of birthdays he has to make up! You can ask for all sorts. What about driving lessons?'

'I'm only thirteen! I don't need them. Our car is about to die anyway.'

'OK, a car then! Designer clothes. A new laptop. Those boots we both want from Bill's Boutique in town. You could get me some too!'

'Are you thinking of all the things *you* want rather than what I would like?' Willow had asked, laughing at Stella's excited face.

'Er, well . . . Yes, because all you're interested in is books! He will be desperate to make it up to you. And he must be loaded. Go on, meet him!'

Willow had known that Stella had been joking but it had tipped her over the edge when she had been dithering in no-man's-land and couldn't decide what to do.

'What's the worst that could happen? You hate him on sight and never have to see him again and life carries on here in the village with us country folk, shunning those city types!' Willow had laughed. 'Go on, you've *always* wondered who he was. And this is your chance to know. Even if you *do* hate him, at least you'll know what he's really like. And you have a brother and a sister too. Something you moan on about not having! Though, to be honest, I don't see what all the fuss is about. Having a brother is soooooo overrated . . . ' That had sealed it. Willow had made her decision.

'I guess I need to meet him to see if I want to be tested for Bella,' she replied to Mum.

Her mum nodded. 'OK, then I need to ring him. He may want to meet today. And that's totally up to you; you can wait till you're really ready. But I don't think that Bella has all the time in the world, if you wanted to be tested, that is. No one says you have to be tested. This is about meeting your . . . father.'

Willow sighed. Of course it was about being tested. That was the only reason Anthony got in contact in this manner—because he wanted her to help him out. Not because he had spent the last thirteen years wondering who she was, feeling too afraid to break the flimsy agreement he and Mum had concocted all those years ago. Willow wasn't fooled by the grown-ups' dressing it up as anything else.

'I'll go and phone him now, shall I?'

Willow nodded and sat down at the kitchen table. Mum disappeared to the living-room to use the landline. Willow drummed her fingers on the table, tapping out an SOS Morse code signal. When that didn't help to calm her down she twisted her hair in her hand and wound it round her finger, pulling it tight till her finger went white.

'What did he say?' Willow asked when Helen returned to the kitchen.

'He wants to come down tomorrow lunchtime.'

Willow felt relieved. At least it gave her time to panic, run around like a headless chicken, and get Stella to give her some slaps and a pep talk. She could imagine Stella going in for the kill: 'I'm Willow's blood donor agent. She ain't signing anything till you deliver the brand new laptop, OK?'

'I said I would check with you.'

Willow just stared at her mum, her mind racing. She spoke after a moment. 'Yes,' she said very quietly. 'I will meet him tomorrow.'

Mum nodded and rang Anthony back immediately, this time on her mobile. They arranged for Anthony to drive down for lunchtime the next day and meet Willow in the small park further up the lane. Helen felt it should be a neutral place and not their home.

'Where will you be, though?' Willow asked anxiously.

'I will be there, right next to you.'

'Mum, won't that be awkward?' Willow asked.

'Er, probably, but it doesn't matter. Would you rather I didn't come?'

'No ... yes. I mean, I want you to be there, but I want to talk to Anthony on my own, I think.'

'OK, how about I walk with you and, when he arrives, come home and you can meet me here afterwards?' Willow nodded. 'And remember to take your phone. If you feel funny, ring me, and I can be there in a jiffy.'

'Mum, can Stella come for a film night tonight because we missed Friday?' Willow really wanted to be distracted from the forthcoming meeting.

'Yes, of course. I've got the ingredients for fajitas. Maybe you can help me chop stuff up later?'

That evening Stella came round with Jarvis. 'Don't worry,' he said as they trudged up the stairs to Willow's room. 'I'll leave before you watch your girlie film. I just wanted to know how you got on with your mum and what you're going to do.'

'What if he kidnaps you and takes you back to London and makes you do the test and then dumps you in a ditch if you're not a match?' Stella gasped when she heard about the plan to meet Anthony in the playground.

'Oh my Lord, Stella. Where do you get these mad ideas from? That would so never happen!' Jarvis said, shaking his head.

'It could!' she replied, jutting out her chin.

'Firstly, he's a famous author so he can't do anything

without it appearing online straight away. Secondly, he doesn't need to dump her in a ditch. Willow isn't a key witness in a murder trial! Thirdly, there will be witnesses to everything.'

'Where?' Stella demanded. 'In the playground? Willow's mum's going to be at home. He could be a mad man and making all this up so he can snatch Willow. Maybe he doesn't have kids; maybe it's all lies.'

'He does have kids, doughnut.'

'For someone who is mega clever, you act a bit dim sometimes,' Willow said, laughing. 'You watch too many rubbish cop shows that are OTT with the drama.'

'It's my escape from my extremely stressful brainiac lifestyle,' Stella concluded, making Willow laugh.

'OK, joking aside, what if Anthony does want to kidnap Willow because he is madly obsessed with finding a donor? She's on her own,' Stella said again.

'Are you fishing for an invite?' Jarvis asked his sister.

'I am actually quite freaked about going on my own,' Willow volunteered.

'We could come!' Stella jumped in. 'We could be your bodyguards.'

Willow shook her head. 'Mum did say she would come, but I feel a bit weird talking to him with her there. But being completely on my own might be even weirder.'

'Then we should be there!' Stella decided. 'We can be your emotional support officers.'

'Why do we have to have a job title?' Jarvis shook his head and groaned.

'Because!' Stella said.

'OK, you guys come to the playground after we arrive. If Mum sees you there, she might get cross. But come later, when she's gone.'

'OK,' Jarvis said. 'Let's work something out and stick to it. You can't be on your own, Willow, if it makes you feel scared.'

When Willow was curled up in her bed sipping her hot chocolate later that evening she felt a lot calmer about the whole meeting. She knew that if Jarvis and Stella were there, backing her up, she would be OK. It had been decided that the twins would be out on their bikes and would wait for Mum to leave the park then zoom in to race round and go on the swings, acting all casual and not at all like stalkers!

Willow tried to imagine how the meeting would go; what Anthony would say. Would he be like Darth Vader in *The Empire Strikes Back* and say, 'Willow, I am your father; you have a sister,' in a very dramatic way, even though she knew all that already? What would he be like? Would he be a cool and trendy dad or one of those sad dads who looked as though they got dressed in the dark? Yes, Mum looked as though she was in a reality TV show called *When Clothes Attack*, but somehow, she wore it well. Mess, chaos, mismatching colours were part of her. Plus she was still very pretty for an ancient grown-up. It hadn't escaped Willow's attention that male teachers and some of the dads at school went bright red when talking to her mum. Mum, being Mum, was oblivious, though. Willow wondered if her mum had ever had a secret boyfriend.

She lay in bed replaying different scenarios and conversations in her head, and even imagining different dads. What if it was obvious Anthony really had no intention of being a dad, and all he was after was her bone marrow? What would she do then? Could she just walk away? Willow tossed and turned until the early hours, unable to sleep. She just wanted the truth to finally be revealed...

Chapter Nine
First impressions

'It's time,' Mum said the next day as she grabbed her house keys and released her best leather biker jacket out of hibernation from the cupboard under the stairs. If Willow hadn't been so nervous she would have poked fun at her mum for making so much effort with her clothes. Mum had washed and dried her hair and it hung shiny and loose without any pencils or glue stuck in it.

Willow and her mum had tried to pretend it was a normal Monday in a normal time, when nothing out of the ordinary was going to happen, and no one was going to have a dramatic soap-opera-like event happen in the park down the lane. Things like this just didn't happen in real life.

As Mum and Willow walked past the twins' gate, Willow glanced over to see her friends sitting on their bikes, looking nonchalantly around as if it was completely normal to be stationary on their bikes in their driveway. She didn't wave and neither did they, not wanting to draw attention to themselves. Stella just gave Willow a very small thumbs up.

Willow smiled to herself and gripped her mum's hand to stop her own from shaking so much.

'Your hands are freezing, peanut. You OK?'

'No, yes, sort of.' Willow had deliberated for ages over what to wear. She too had washed and dried her hair so it was all neat and less like a bird's nest. She chose jeans and a red jumper dress over the top with her ankle boots and denim jacket. She didn't want to be shivering in the park.

It was one o'clock, the time they had asked Anthony to come to the playground. They turned the corner and opened the green metal gate which gave the customary squeaky groan. The playground had a small adjacent car park to the right as you looked at it and a small wooden community centre that was in need of some TLC and a new roof. There was a low hedge which divided the car park and the community centre from the park. The playground was straight ahead with swings, slides, a sick-inducing roundabout, and a zip wire, and behind that was a skate park and picnic area.

'He's not here,' Mum said, noting the absence of any parked cars. But just then a black people carrier pulled up. It stopped and the driver's door opened. A man got out, stretched, and checked his watch. 'That's him,' Mum said with conviction. She waved Anthony over. He locked the car and, finding the gap in the hedge, walked towards them, almost tripping over on his way.

Willow swallowed hard, regretting eating the toast she'd had earlier. Mum gripped her hand tight. 'It'll be OK, peanut. Just you see.' Was that for Willow or for her own benefit? Willow wondered. All she knew was that her feet felt as though they were made of lead and her head could at any moment spontaneously combust with all the thoughts and planned conversations overloading her brain.

Watching her dad it was obvious to Willow that he was a cool type, or at least he got dressed with the light on and made an effort. He was wearing a V-necked navy jumper with a white T-shirt poking out at the top, nice jeans, trainers, and a trendy-looking black anorak bomber jacket. He was 'put together', as Granna would say. His salt-and-pepper black hair was collar length, just like in his picture.

'Hello, Helen,' Anthony said and immediately dropped his car keys on the floor. He bent down to pick them up. When he stood up he took Willow's mum's hand and kissed her on both cheeks. 'You look the same as ever. The age fairy didn't get you then.'

'I wish,' Mum replied, more guarded. 'You look very well. Grey hair suits you.'

'You must be Willow,' Anthony turned to her. 'Thank you for agreeing to meet with me.' He didn't lean in to kiss her but he held his hand out and she tentatively took it.

Willow could feel it shaking in her grip and she looked up at him. He was biting his lip, nervously. Good, Willow thought. He should be nervous!

'How long did it take you to get down here?' Mum asked, kicking off the small talk.

'About two and a half hours. Not too bad.' Willow looked at her mum and dad, now strangers to each other and tried to imagine them in love, laughing, holding hands, planning their future together, and she couldn't see it. Probably because she was used to her mum just being her mum and nobody's girlfriend or wife. If Willow could imagine any man for her mum, she would have imagined an artist or someone vaguely madcap. From first impressions, Anthony was normal.

'Listen, I'm going to go home. Willow, give me a ring whenever—you know.' She gave her daughter a hug. 'I'll see you later, Anthony.'

'Yes, bye. Thank you again.'

Willow watched her mum head back through the gate and out onto the lane back home, past the twins' house. They would be here in a minute to take over.

'So . . . where do you want to go? Do you want to sit down?' Anthony nodded at the benches in the field past the skate park. Willow looked at his hands; they were still shaking.

'OK,' Willow said. This was so odd it just didn't feel real. Friday morning, her father was still an anonymous sperm donor and now, three days later, he was here in front of her, asking if she wanted to go and sit down at a picnic bench in the park she had been coming to for as long as she could remember.

'Is this where you and your friends hang out then?' Anthony asked awkwardly, as they made their way towards the picnic area.

'Sometimes,' Willow answered. How was she supposed to behave? She didn't know. She wanted to rage at him for not having anything to do with her all these years and suddenly expecting her to help his dying daughter. It was so confusing. As Anthony groped around for a conversation opener, the twins suddenly skidded into the park, looking around for her. They spotted Willow just as she sat down opposite her dad at the nearest bench to the skate park. Buoyed up by their appearance, Willow suddenly knew just what she wanted to do. She would ask the difficult truthful questions because someone had to. She noticed how grown-ups had a tendency to start off slowly with small talk instead of getting right in there. Why wait? No one cares about the weather, Willow wanted to scream. Or how easy it was to get a seat on the train. Just say what you mean! 'Anthony?'

'Yes, Willow.' He seemed relieved that Willow had started the ball rolling.

'Don't you think it's a bit rubbish that after all these years of not wanting anything to do with me, you suddenly track me down and want my help?' She jutted her chin out at him and thought she was going to faint from the confrontation and crossness bubbling away in her belly. Uh-oh, she was on a roll. She had opened Pandora's box and now all the inky black truths were flying out: 'I mean, is it coincidence that it's taken you thirteen years to work up the courage to barge into my life just when your daughter is sick and might need my bone marrow? Not thought about saying hi before now?!' Willow was furious all of a sudden; much more than she had been with her mum when she'd finally told her the truth.

Anthony seemed floored, a bit like being punched with a left hook in a boxing fight when you were expecting a right. He stood up and looked as though he was going to walk off. Had Willow pushed too far on their first encounter?

Chapter Ten
The twins stand guard

'Wow! What an opener,' Anthony said in a choked voice from his standing position. He walked shakily round the picnic bench and perched on the very edge of the same bench as Willow. There was a look of total admiration in his eyes as he faced his daughter defiantly challenging him, along with a hint of sadness too. 'I don't know how to come back after that,' he said.

Willow continued to stare at him because she didn't know what to do or say either. He took a deep breath.

'Yes, Willow. It is a bit rubbish. In fact, it's more than rubbish. Your mum already very kindly pointed that out to me when she rang me yesterday . . . Did your mum tell you about us and what happened in the past?'

'Yes. She told me you both agreed to have no contact after I was born and that you would send money.'

'When you put it like that it sounds almost callous,' Anthony said quietly.

'Granna said she sent you a picture of me when I was born and never heard anything ever again.'

'No.' Anthony looked as though he was struggling to find the right words. He looked down at his hands.

'I know you and Mum said no contact, but did that *really* mean no contact? Like you didn't want photos, to hear about school reports, how I was getting on. Anything at all?'

Anthony sat there quietly for a moment. Eventually he made eye contact and said, 'Willow, I can't make up to you everything that has happened. I really am truly sorry you have had to find out about me and the reason I never got in contact until now. And you may not believe anything I say to you, but the day you were born was a difficult day. When Lillian sent that picture to my office I wanted to turn up at her house and say "to hell with the agreement, I want to see my daughter!"' Anthony's eyes misted over for a second and then he looked directly at Willow. 'I still have it at work, hidden away in a drawer. I look at it every year on your birthday and all days in between.'

'Why didn't you just turn up, then?'

Anthony looked shamefaced and he bit his lip. 'Because I was scared.'

'Of a baby? Of me?' Willow didn't understand.

'Of everything. Of telling my wife I had a secret daughter. Of how mad, upset, betrayed she would feel.'

'But what about what I would feel?' Willow asked, in a small voice.

Anthony looked as though she had just stabbed him and twisted a knife in his gut. He took another deep breath as if to steady his voice. 'Willow, selfishly I couldn't think about how you would feel because if I had done, that would have been it. I would have hammered down Lillian's door and begged to be a part of your life. I knew if I started getting reports and pictures, news of what you were up to, that I wouldn't be able to stay away. That I would want to be involved, and the deal was that I wouldn't get involved. That I would be hands off. I couldn't risk hurting my family by telling them about you at any point since you were born. And the longer it went on without anyone knowing about you, the harder it became to just casually drop you into conversation.'

'But you're willing to hurt them now?' Willow questioned, put out that she was seen as a 'problem'. 'Or are you not going to tell them about me?' She didn't know where her strength to ask such difficult questions was coming from. 'Do they know about me already?'

Anthony squirmed in his seat. 'No, they don't know about you. Not yet. I'm going to tell them tonight.'

Anthony turned to look at Willow directly in the eyes, a dramatic flush creeping from right under his chin, making it look as though he had been sunbathing for too long, with white patches round his eyes where his shades would have been. 'When Bella was born you would have been about two. I went into a deep depression because when I held her in my arms for the first time all I could think about was you. I wondered what you were doing, if you were talking, if you were happy, who you looked like. I felt as though something was missing.' Willow was sad; she could tell he wasn't lying. She too experienced the missing feeling occasionally. Anthony's eyes were glistening with tears. 'And I almost cracked and got hold of your grandma.' He stopped and took a deep breath and exhaled heavily, as though it was the first time he had ever said that out loud.

'And? Did you?' Willow enquired, not sure whether he had or not and whether Mum had covered it up.

'No, I'm sorry to say I didn't. The low point passed, but that didn't mean I didn't stop thinking about you.' Anthony was twisting his gold wedding ring round and round on his finger as he talked.

The fight left Willow's body and she slumped against the back of the bench. Unsure about what to say next, she stared at the twins. They were looking over at her from the skate park. 'Please can I see a picture of Bella and Archie?' she asked, feeling it was the right thing to say. That was why they were here after all.

'Yes, yes, of course!' Anthony visibly brightened at the chance to change the subject. He got out his wallet and his phone and passed her a school photo of them both. 'I have more on my phone that you can see. That's the most recent one of them both before Bella got sick.' Out of the picture smiled two younger children.

'How old is Archie?' Willow asked.

'Just seven.'

Bella was pretty with a heart-shaped face. Her eyes were quite intense and she was very pale with dark shoulder-length wavy hair. She didn't look like Anthony at all, but the little boy did. He was a mini-me of Anthony, even down to the surfer-boy hair, except his wasn't salt-and-pepper, of course. Anthony handed Willow his phone and she scrolled through some photos, Anthony pointing out where they were, what they were doing, and how old Bella and Archie were when the pictures were taken. She saw pictures of Maria, his wife, too, and remembered her face from the internet when she and the twins had sneaked a look. She scrolled past a few pictures of Anthony snuggling Bella or Archie and some of the whole family lying flat on the floor, Anthony holding the camera away from them and taking a group shot. Willow wondered what it would be like for her to be in those photos too, to be part of the family. . .

'How did Bella get sick?' Willow asked.

'No one knows. She had been feeling tired and achy for a while. She had a sore throat that wouldn't go away, no matter how many antibiotics the doctor prescribed her. One day she came back from school with a few horrible bruises on her legs and arms and we thought she had been beaten up and was keeping quiet about it, but she said not. Then the final warning was at taekwondo. After a class a few months ago she collapsed of exhaustion and, where she had been sparring with another child, with pads on, her leg was really bruised. Maria took her to the doctor who rushed her to hospital where we found out that she had very severe aplastic anaemia.'

'Yes, I looked it up on the internet,' Willow said.

'The only cure is to have a bone marrow transplant at this stage. None of us was a match and you know the rest . . . ' Willow could feel his despair hanging in the air between them.

'So the reason you wanted to see me was to ask for my help. To see if I would be tested as a match for Bella?'

'Yes. I'm aware of how mercenary this looks to you. I could attempt to disguise my original intentions, but you're too smart and that wouldn't be right. I need your help, Willow. Bella needs your help. We are running out of time and chances.'

Willow looked at her dad. She knew she had the power to break him if she wanted to, to take revenge for abandoning her as a baby. But that would be cruel. She couldn't do it, not now she had seen the face of her sister smiling innocently out of the photos. Even having the thought made her shudder inside. 'I'll be tested,' she said.

Anthony shuffled up the bench and grabbed her hands, the first proper physical contact other than their formal handshake. 'Thank you, Willow. You have no idea how much this means to me.'

Willow blushed bright red and looked down at her lap, shrugging him off at the same time. 'S'OK. What do I have to do?'

'You'll need to come up to London and have a blood test, or maybe your doctor can do it here and send it up to Bella's hospital. I will check with Maria and ask Helen if this is all OK.' Anthony looked as though he would have happily taken the blood sample there and then.

'Have you had any lunch?' Anthony asked.

Willow shook her head. Lunch had been the last thing on her mind earlier.

'Would you like me to take you out somewhere? Do you have tea rooms or a café round here where you can get food? I didn't eat either and I'm starving now.'

Willow didn't know what she wanted to do.

'No pressure. If you would rather just go home, we can go out for lunch next time if you like. You haven't told me anything about you.' Next time? That sounded so weird. Going out for lunch with her dad. She would never have thought it in a million years.

'OK, next time,' Willow said, relieved. She wanted him to go now so she could talk to the twins.

'Here's my card. Ring me any time you need to. If I don't pick up I'll ring you straight back, I promise.' And he handed her a business card with his name and mobile number on it. The background of the card had a shadowy design of an old fashioned typewriter with the black shiny text printed over the top. 'Tell your mum I'll ring her this evening and we can sort out another meeting.' He stood up and so did Willow. 'Do you want a lift home?'

'Nah. I'm good, thanks. I'll walk. It's only just down there.' They started walking back towards the entrance of the park.

'Thank you, Willow. I'm so grateful that you agreed to come here today. I really enjoyed meeting you.' And before she could do anything, he leaned down and kissed her on the cheek. He smelled of soap and vaguely of something else—man perfume, perhaps. 'I'll see you very soon.' And he smiled at her.

'Yes, bye . . . '

As he walked back over to his car, the twins circled the grassy bit where Willow was standing, waiting for the car to leave before they came over and grilled her. Anthony waved goodbye and his car disappeared in the direction of the village green.

The twins finally swerved in front of Willow. 'Come on, then. What happened?' Stella asked, unable to contain herself any more. 'Is he going to pay you loads of money for helping him out?'

'Stella!' Willow exclaimed. 'Of course he isn't.' Willow was so relieved it was over but her heart was still pounding in her ears. She felt like a boxed racehorse on the start line, jittery and hyper.

'Bet you wished you had asked him to though now, don't you?' she said jokingly. 'I should have told you to ask before you met up! I should be your agent!'

Willow pushed her off her bike and jumped on, racing back to the skate park with Stella chasing her, dirt all over her nice jeans where she had fallen over.

'I'm going to kill you, Wilhelmina!'

Jarvis sighed and rolled his eyes. 'You two, stop it. Just tell us what happened. I want to know!'

Chapter Eleven
A trip to London

'Which train is it?' Willow squinted at the electronic announcement board.

'The one to Victoria.' It was ten o'clock in the morning, the day after Willow and Anthony's meeting at the park. In the end the hospital said they wanted Willow to come to them, so Mum had got them on the first train after rush hour. Anthony said he would reimburse them for all travel expenses and anything else they needed. He probably would have paid for a limo if they had asked.

Willow and her mum sat on the train, both with a window seat opposite each other. Willow watched the fields flash past, broken intermittently by telegraph poles or houses. They barely spoke, Willow lost in her own thoughts, while her mum attempted to read a trashy magazine.

After a while Mum broke the silence. 'Are you OK, peanut?'

'Will I have to meet Bella, Archie, and Maria today too?' Willow asked warily.

'No, not at all. It will just be us, Anthony, and the doctor.'

'When will I have to meet them?'

'I don't know. Anthony was telling them all last night. So, depending on how that goes down, it could be sooner rather than later. But again, if you're not sure, you can wait as long as you like.'

Willow sighed. She wanted to meet Archie and Bella, but not yet. This was all too soon for her; she wasn't ready. And as for Maria, she was a bit scared of meeting her. What if she hated her and thought bad stuff about Willow and her mum? Willow's mind was racing with all sorts of thoughts. What if Bella hated her? Anthony hadn't mentioned what sort of girl she was. What if they just didn't get on, like Amy and Jo in *Little Women*?

As the fields morphed into houses and then offices, the hour-and-a-half journey drew to a close. Willow's mum came into town fairly regularly for meetings with galleries and the record company, but Willow had only been up a few times with her mum, and once with her school to the Imperial War Museum. The busyness of Victoria Station threw her off-kilter. It made her village seem even more like Hicksville. It was hectic, with people dancing round each other with huge coffin-like suitcases on wheels, briefcases, holdalls, and backpacks.

'Come on, Willow, stop gawping. We've got to go on the Underground now.'

Willow found the maze of tunnels and walkways to get to the right Tube train even more confusing and hectic than the station concourse above.

'Quick, here's our train, hop on!' It wasn't so busy on the platform and they managed to get on the Tube without getting pushed onto the tracks. Something Willow was trying not to think about.

'How do you even know this is the right train? There're no clues. I would so get lost if I was on my own.'

'Good job you're not on your own then, isn't it?' Mum said, squeezing her hand. 'I used to go on the Tube all the time when Anthony and I lived in London.'

'Where did you live?'

'For a while we lived in a tiny flat in Waterloo, right near the station. It was above a pizza delivery place. So the living room smelled of pizza all the time. It could have been worse; it could have been a fish and chip shop.'

'Were you poor?'

'No, but we didn't have much money. Anthony managed to get us nights out on expenses and there were free restaurant openings and stuff like that. It was fun.' Willow found it hard to imagine her mum having fun with her dad. It felt as though Mum was talking about a couple of strangers.

'Look, our stop.' The train ground to a halt. 'We're going to be on time for a change.' Mum stood up and grabbed Willow's hand and they jumped down from the train. Once outside the Tube entrance and on the high street, Mum turned and faced Willow. 'Now, I just want to say something. You have every right to change your mind, even at the last minute. No one will be cross. Anthony said you can maybe talk to a counsellor today and the nurse might ask you some questions about whether you are OK to go ahead with this. I've had a word with Anthony and told him no coercing and no bribery if you say no.'

'Bang goes my dream of a pony, then,' Willow joked nervously.

'This is a massive thing you are doing today. It's not just about whether you are a match or not; your life is going to be different from now on. You're not going to be Willow with a sperm donor as a dad, you're going to be Willow with a dad, a step-mum and a brother and a sister.'

'And a mum, a real mum!' Willow protested.

Yes, I am your mum, silly.' Mum fiercely hugged Willow, holding her close. 'Are you ready? Shall we go?'

Willow nodded. She felt as though she had only just realized this was actually happening; being jabbed with a needle. They were going to take blood; it would be sucked it out of her arm. Willow inhaled deeply as she walked, her legs feeling like jelly, trying to block the image of blood and needles from her pounding head. Had she really thought this through? Could she actually do it without fainting and smashing her head open all over again?

Chapter Twelve
It's just a scratch

'Willow, Helen!' Anthony looked like a man possessed as he practically ambushed them from behind a pot plant right near the entrance to the hospital. He looked as though he had slept in his clothes. His jumper was crumpled like a scrunched piece of paper flattened out and he looked slightly dishevelled; his hair was sticking up on one side and his eyes were red.

'Are you OK?' Mum asked. 'You don't look it.'

'It didn't go that . . . smoothly, telling Maria about Willow.' He smiled weakly at them, the smile never reaching his eyes. 'Do you guys want anything? Coffee, tea, juice, cakes?'

'Great! I knew she would hate me!' Willow said, dismayed.

Anthony looked horrified. 'No, no, I don't want you to say that. If there's anyone she hates right now it's me, for keeping you a secret all these years.'

'Oh.'

'Yes, she was very . . . er, disgruntled that I never told her in the first place.'

'She would have been OK about it all?' Mum asked.

'So she says. She feels very hurt that I would think otherwise. And the fact that I was so cloak-and-dagger about Willow.'

Willow felt a huge wave of relief. She could tell that what had happened last night wasn't great for Anthony, but for her it was good news: Maria didn't hate her and that meant she didn't feel so sick at the thought of meeting her. Then she had another thought: 'So . . . if Maria would have been OK with the idea of me, you know, being around, then none of this . . . lying . . . needed to have happened!'

Her mum and Anthony looked incredibly shifty. 'Anthony, over to you?' Mum said as they hovered in the foyer.

'I don't know what to say. It's more complicated than that . . . '

Willow looked at her Mum and then at Anthony and shook her head. 'What is it with grown-ups? Why does it always have to be "complicated"?'

Anthony burst out laughing. 'You're totally right. I have no idea!'

'Listen, why don't we grab a coffee?' Mum said, spotting a café. 'Do we have time?'

'Yes, yes. I'm in need of a caffeine injection myself,' Anthony admitted, delving in his pockets for his wallet. 'Willow, what would you like?'

'I'm good, thanks.' Anthony's mere mention of the word 'injection' set Willow off again, scared she would puke up there and then in the lobby before they had even made it upstairs for the actual real event.

'I'll take you up to the kids' unit where a nurse will take blood,' Anthony said, once they had emerged from the cafe with their takeaway coffees.

The word 'blood' made Willow feel even more dizzy and she had to pull herself together. Man up! she told herself. We've not even made it out of the lobby yet! But her sweaty top lip gave the game away.

The outside of the hospital was Victorian and severe-looking but the inside was modern and light and not at all scary. Anthony took them in a lift, down corridors and into the kids' brightly decorated unit that looked more like a cool and trendy hotel than a hospital. There were ridiculously massive photos of street graffiti blown up and plastered on the curved walls, acid-yellow and pink panels lined the corridors, and the sofas in reception could have been out of a *Beautiful Homes* magazine. Willow liked it at once. She had imagined it would be a replica of all the hospital dramas she had seen on TV: dark, hectic people running this way and that, pushing half-dead people on trolleys. Instead it was an oasis of calm and no one was running around anywhere. In fact, where were all the people?

The ultra-modern reception desk boasted the kind of curved wooden exterior that you might see in a five-star hotel and the receptionists sat on black leather swivel chairs that looked as if they could have come from a James Bond film. One of the women behind the desk smiled at Anthony. 'Hello there, what can we do for you today?'

'This is Willow Fitzpatrick. Claire Fredericks is going to take her blood,' Anthony replied. The receptionist, whose name badge said she was called Rosa, nodded and picked up the phone to call the nurse into reception.

Willow sat down on the sofa. It wasn't as comfy as it appeared. It needed to be jumped on to loosen it up a bit. Mum stood at the desk for a few minutes, sipping her takeaway coffee with Anthony, looking around, then came and sat down with Willow. Anthony soon followed. 'Claire's going to be a few minutes,' she said, patting Willow's knee.

'Where's Bella's ward?' Willow asked.

'Bella isn't in hospital yet; she's still at home. She'll come into hospital to have chemotherapy if . . . when she has the bone marrow transplant,' said Anthony.

'Does she know about me yet?'

'No. The doctors do. And so does Maria. We are going to see if you are a match first before we introduce you to her.'

Willow looked visibly relieved. The thought of bumping into Bella had been worrying her more than she had realized.

'But you will tell her, eventually, won't you?' Mum bristled slightly.

'Yes, of course. We aren't not going to introduce you if you aren't a match. We just thought that all introductions should wait till after the blood-test result, that's all. I don't want Bella to get her hopes up about a donor again . . . '

Just then Willow spotted a nurse walking towards them. Anthony stood up, along with Willow and her mum.

'Hi, Anthony. You must be Helen and Willow. Very pleased to meet you,' she said, extending her hand first to Mum and then to Willow. 'My name is Claire. Please follow me.' Claire was really young with blonde hair in a ponytail and didn't look much like a nurse; she was just wearing normal clothes with an apron over the top.

They followed her past reception and down the acid-yellow corridor with framed cool artwork on the walls. She took them past what looked like a lounge area and then they stopped outside a door. She opened it and sunlight flooded in from the large window by the desk.

'Take a seat, guys.' Claire sat at the desk and gestured for them to take one of the three chairs on the other side. 'Now, Willow, I'm slightly concerned about taking your blood today.'

'Why?' All three of them asked in unison.

'Because normally we would have had time to talk this through and if you had wanted to talk to a psychologist we would have arranged that.' Claire paused and looked at each of them, hard. 'This is an extremely unorthodox case. You've only just found out who your father is and that you have a sick sister you never knew existed. It is rather a lot for you to take in. And then throw into the mix donating your bone marrow to the previously mentioned sick sister. It's all rather complicated, isn't it?'

Anthony looked slightly panic-stricken at Claire's appraisal of the situation.

'What do you think, Willow?' Mum asked her.

Willow shrugged. That word 'complicated' reared its head again. All this asking her what she thought wasn't really useful to her because she didn't know.

'Are you happy to be tested to see if you're a match for Bella?' Claire asked her gently.

'Yes. I want to be tested.' And she gave Claire a weak smile.

'And you know that there's only a small chance you

might be a match. So please don't feel bad if it doesn't work out; it's not your fault.' Willow nodded. 'Have you got any questions you would like to ask me?'

Willow thought for a moment. She had been pondering this on the way up on the train. 'Yes, how long until I know whether I am a match or not?'

'It will take about two weeks to get the result back from the lab.'

'And then what happens if I am? How soon do I come to hospital and where will I be?'

'Well, say you are a match, we'll ring you and let you know. Then, as soon as Bella is ready to receive your donation, you will come up here in this unit and have the bone marrow harvested the next day.'

'Will Mum be able to stay here?'

'Of course. We have beds for parents. But you won't have to stay in hospital very long. Only two days. Most kids are OK to go home twenty-four hours after the operation.'

'Will it hurt?' Willow asked nervously.

'You shouldn't be in too much pain,' Claire said kindly. 'There may be some stiffness in your back or pain where the puncture wounds are, but we can give painkillers for that.'

'How long will the operation take?' Mum asked, sounding a bit jittery.

'About an hour and a half.'

Willow tried to get her head around having an operation and found that she couldn't comprehend the gravity of it.

'Right, shall we take some blood then?' Claire asked, clapping her hands together and opening the desk drawer to find her supply of needles.

'Can you roll your left sleeve up and make your left hand into a fist? Pump your fist for me.' Willow eyed the needle suspiciously as Claire ripped down the side of the sterile packet. She was already feeling queasy at the mention of puncture wounds.

'Look at me, peanut, so you're distracted,' Mum instructed, taking hold of her other hand.

'You'll just feel a little scratch,' Claire said as she stuck the needle into Willow's arm. Willow felt light-headed and looked at Anthony, who smiled at her. 'Almost done . . . '

Willow went deaf and felt her hands and feet turn cold, like ice.

'All done!' Claire said happily.

Willow made the mistake of looking too soon just as Claire was taking the needle out of the crook of her arm with the vial of blood right there.

Willow felt all the blood rush from her head and a

furious cold sweat break out on her face and body. Any minute now she knew she was going to be sick and the only thing she could do to stop it was drop her head down between her legs.

'Willow!' she heard her mum shout. She felt a hand on her back and then nothing. Everything went black.

'Willow, peanut . . . ' Willow sat up very slowly, blinking, and looked at her mum who was on her haunches in front of her, rubbing one of her hands and looking very worried. Her head was throbbing, the pain right behind her eyes. Her mouth felt like the bottom of a hamster cage and she gladly took the water that her mum was offering her. Her hand was a bit shaky and water slopped over the side and dropped onto her jeans.

'Are you OK?' Mum asked, sitting back on her chair next to Willow. 'You passed out.'

Willow nodded, unable to speak.

'Deep breaths,' Claire said. 'Get the oxygen flowing again.'

'I didn't know there was a possibility you would faint,' Anthony said, sounding anguished.

'I don't like needles or blood,' Willow explained slowly in between deep breaths. 'They make me feel really sick.'

'You should have said!' Anthony exclaimed.

'Why? I still had to do it.'

'Thank you so much, Willow.' He looked properly impressed. 'I can't believe you went through with that even though you've got a phobia. This must be like your worst nightmare. I'm taking you out for lunch now, whatever you want! Though of course that's nothing compared to what you've just done!'

'In that case I'd like a pony, please.' They all looked at her.

'Er, of course. If that's what you really want.'

'Don't be stupid! I was kidding. Checking to see if you would give me whatever I wanted!' Willow even managed a little giggle, the headache easing off and the blood gradually returning to all the right places. 'A pizza will do fine.'

Anthony, Mum, and Claire burst out laughing. 'Glad to see you still have your sense of humour intact,' her mum joked with Willow. 'Are you sure you will be able to eat anything? You still look very pale.'

'I'll be OK in a bit, Mum. At least I didn't bang my head this time!'

When Willow was able to stand up and walk without wobbling, Anthony shook hands with Claire and they left the room while Claire parcelled up the blood.

'Right, pizza it is then!' Anthony said. 'I know just the place.' Willow and Mum followed Anthony through the maze of corridors and out into the real world.

So this is it, Willow thought as they stood on the pavement while Anthony flagged down a black cab. The first proper lunch with Mum and my dad. What if he and Mum just don't get on? What if I don't like him once we have a proper chat? What if he chews his food in a weird way so that it makes me feel sick?

Willow just wanted to go home now, back to the safety of her village, where it was just Mum, Granna, and the twins and no one did anything out of the ordinary. Like have lunch with their famous father they never knew existed . . .

Chapter Thirteen
Lunch with Mum and Dad!

Anthony took them to a small Italian restaurant in a side street near Selfridges, the department store. 'They do the best pizzas I've ever had!' he told them as they sat down underneath spidery hanging baskets filled with bright green ferns.

The restaurant played the kind of music you would expect to hear on holiday, in Italy: folksy and traditional. Willow liked it.

Willow was totally ravenous and forgot her nerves as soon as the delicious smell of pizza wafted up her nostrils. She was so hungry that she would have eaten the menu had it been smothered in cheese! Instead she settled for devouring all of the breadsticks. 'I didn't want any breadsticks anyway,' Mum teased after they had ordered their pizzas.

As they waited for the food, Anthony launched into a barrage of questions for Willow. 'So, Willow, who is your best friend?'

'Stella from next door. She has a twin brother,

101

Jarvis, and he kind of comes as part of the package with Stella!'

'Were they the guys on the bikes who zoomed over after I got in the car?'

'Er, yes.' Mum looked at her quizzically but let it go.

'Were they checking up on me?'

'Sort of. They wanted to be there in case you tried to kidnap me. Stella had a warning whistle and everything.'

'Only Stella could think up something as mad as that,' her mum sighed. 'I'm assuming it was Stella and not you?' Willow nodded, smiling at the lunacy of it all.

'Well, I hope you've realized I'm not going to kidnap you.' Anthony looked a bit uncomfortable. 'So, what's your favourite subject at school?'

'English; I love writing stories.'

'Ah! Yes, your mum told me. I thought maybe you would like this.' And he bent down to where he'd left his satchel under the table. He drew out a crushed posh paper bag with handles and handed it to Willow.

She peered inside and delved in, pulling out a really beautiful cloth-bound book. The cloth looked like silk with red ribbons woven through the turquoise, rainbow shimmery fabric. It was magical and reminded her of a spell book from an old-fashioned fairytale.

'Oh wow!' Willow breathed. She opened it up inside, to an ocean of blank pages. No lines, just empty space that needed to be filled with ideas, jottings, lists, and dreams. 'I love it! Thank you!'

'I got you plain paper as I like to have my ideas books completely blank so I can write as big or small as I like. I thought you might like the same.' Willow nodded. 'There's something else in there.'

Willow peered into the depths of the bag and spotted a small slimline black box. She picked it out with her fingertips. She placed it on the table and carefully lifted off the lid. Inside was a gold pen. Willow took it out of its protective box and turned it round in the candle light. It sparkled and shone. On one side was an engraving: *Willow's pen for writing magic.*

'It's a fountain pen. All the top writers use them.' Anthony smiled at her as she popped off the lid to inspect the nib. He slid a big box of cartridges across the table to her.

'Thank you. It's beautiful.'

'No, thank *you*. I wanted to get you that pony, but thought it might look a bit crass, like I was bribing you,' Anthony replied, half joking.

'Well, aren't you?' Willow said cheekily, laughing at his obvious discomfort.

'No! If I was going to bribe you I would have gone bigger, but I think your mum would have had something to say about that!'

Mum nodded. 'Yes, I had strict words: nothing flash just yet.'

'Mum! Don't ruin my chances of bagging some loot!'

'Joking aside, Willow, I really can't stress how sorry I am, about everything. I want to make it up to you. And I totally appreciate that you agreed to be tested, even though you hate needles. I can't believe you did that for us. I am really touched.'

Willow shifted in her seat, embarrassed. Luckily the pizzas arrived at that exact moment and everyone busied themselves with eating and ooohing at the deliciousness of the food.

'What do you write about?' Anthony asked, once they had all slowed down a bit.

'Anything—whatever the teacher asks us to, but stuff that happens to me as well. I'm being entered for a competition by the school.' Willow blushed as she never normally boasted about anything. It was easy to forget her dad was an author and quite famous.

'Tell me more . . . ' So Willow talked about school, Mrs Bannister, *Little Women,* and how she got round to being entered for the writing competition. As Willow finished up the last mouthful of pizza, Anthony said, 'When you get back home I'd love you to send me some of your writing, if you wouldn't mind?' Willow nodded and blushed again. What if he thought she was rubbish?

After lunch Anthony said goodbye and asked if they wanted a cab to the station, which Mum said no to. She wanted to take Willow to the National Portrait Gallery and Trafalgar Square. 'I'll ring you guys tomorrow, then. OK? Thank you so much. What you did today means a lot.' And he disappeared off into the crowds towards the Tube.

'Mum?' Willow said as they vegetated on the sofa at home later that evening.

'Yep.'

'Did Anthony ever actually ask you to marry him on a bended knee, properly?' Willow asked, expecting her mum to shout, "No!" '

Mum was silent for a moment.

'Sort of.'

'What does that mean?' Willow was incredulous.

'He did ask me.'

'How?'

'It was on holiday, in Greece. On a small island we had discovered when we were island-hopping one year.'

'And . . . ? When?'

'I was twenty-seven, so three years before we split up.'

'Were you still in love with him then?'

'Oh yes, madly.'

'So why did you say no?'

'I didn't.'

'Oh . . . Tell me, please!' Mum grimaced. 'Please, Mum. I really want to know.'

Mum took a deep breath. 'He asked me on a bended knee, taking me totally by surprise, at the edge of the sea in Greece.'

'What did you say?' Willow breathed.

'I told him to get up because he was getting soaked. And he said, "Not until you give me an answer." ' She paused.

'And . . . ?'

'And I said, "Yes. Yes, I will marry you! Get up!" So he did.'

'Did he get you a ring?'

Mum pulled her silver chain from around her neck. On it there was a Virgin Mary pendant, a silver heart, a delicate pair of silver angel wings, and a silver ring with a flat round blue stone mounted on it. She found the clasp of the chain at the back of her neck and undid it. She slid the ring off and gave it to Willow. 'You have it. It was just a cheap silver ring from one of the market stalls. I don't know why I kept it all these years. Maybe deep down I knew I was supposed to give it to you in the end.'

'Are you sure?' She knew she had a spare chain upstairs that it could hang on until it fitted properly.

Her mum nodded. 'Come on, enough of my trip down memory lane. It's late and I'm shattered. Bed.'

Willow heaved herself up from the sofa, kissed her mum, and asked one last question. 'Did you really want to marry Anthony?'

'Maybe. I don't know. We wanted different things. I'm not really the marrying kind!'

Willow laughed. That was something she definitely knew for sure!

Chapter Fourteen
Another day trip

'Willow?' Mum's voice punctured the stillness of the garden where Willow was sitting on a deckchair, reading a book Anthony had sent her after their last meeting—*Good Wives*, the follow-up to *Little Women*. He had written on the title page:

I hope this helps you with your writing project. It's always good to read more of what you love.

Anthony x

'Anthony just rang. They've told Bella about you.'

'Oh . . . ' Willow's stomach did a harsh nosedive to her feet and she put the book down on her lap. 'What did she say?' Willow wasn't sure she wanted to know.

'He didn't let on. But he thinks it would be a good idea for us to visit this Saturday if you would postpone your shopping day out with the gang. Apparently Archie is dying to meet you!'

Willow groaned quietly. She had been looking forward to Saturday for ages. It was what had kept her going when it felt like all her friends seemed to be away. Being an only child definitely had its downsides, though Stella would always disagree with her on that one when she moaned about it! Stella and Jarvis had been away at their grandparents since Willow had had her blood test and Willow had had to be satisfied with almost hourly texts from Stella to make up for her absence.

'OK,' she agreed after a moment. Her mum came over and hugged her.

'Thank you, peanut. I know it's annoying and you've had this planned for ages, but this is important.'

'I know, Mum. But why did they tell her about me? We don't know whether I'm a match yet.'

'The doctors didn't want it being a total shock to her, finding out she had a sister just before her chemo started, if you were a match, that is.'

'Right.' Willow didn't know what to say. She felt upset that she could cause a shock, though she totally knew that's what her existence would be to Bella. After all, she had been lied to just as much as Willow, and would probably freak out just as she had done.

'They want her to respond to the treatment in a positive way and just want to get her used to the idea of you first. They had to tell her sometime, so it may as well be now.' Mum patted her knee. 'It is a big shock, peanut. She hasn't had to share her daddy with anyone apart from Archie, and suddenly you turn up. She's very sick too, remember. It's a lot to take in.'

'I know,' Willow sighed, feeling bad that she had felt upset.

'Why don't you go and ring Stella and see if you can rearrange the day out so you can go?' Willow nodded and got up from the deckchair and went inside to find her phone.

'Wilhemina! What's up? Not texted you for about five minutes. How're those little women?'

'Still little. Listen, I need to ask you something.'

'Uh-oh, sounds ominous. Jarvis is doing my nut, as if you hadn't guessed. Wants me to listen to him droning on about boring computers. I have been banging my head against a brick wall to dull the pain.'

'Can we change the date of the day out on Saturday?' Willow butted in while Stella took a breath in her rant against Jarvis.

'Not really. It's the only day everyone can make.' Stella sounded slightly put out.

'I can't make it. I have to go to London to meet Bella and Archie.'

Stella remained silent, which Willow knew was a rare occurrence for her.

'Stella?'

'Yes, sorry. You told me you were only meeting her after you found out if you were a match or not. So you're having the operation?'

'No, no! They just want me to meet her now instead.'

'Phew, I thought you were about to go missing in action having an op and I wouldn't see you before it.'

'No, we still don't know anything yet.'

'Well, I'm sorry we can't change the day out,' Stella said, sounding a bit flat. 'Look, I've got to go, Grandma is flapping her hands at me. Either she's trying to fly or we're going out. Listen, good luck with Bella and Archie. I hope you're OK. Text me what happens!'

Willow nodded and said goodbye. Her eyes pricked with tears and she brushed them away. She knew she couldn't expect everyone to change their day out because of her, but it still hurt when Stella didn't even say she would ask everyone and see if they could. She'd also wanted to talk to Stella about how she felt Bella wasn't looking forward to meeting her because Mum only mentioned that Archie was excited. She felt very

111

alone inside her head all of a sudden. Everyone would be having fun in town, having a laugh on Saturday, and what would she be doing? Having one of the biggest meetings of her life and yet again she had no idea how it was going to go. Willow hoped Bella might be a *bit* excited to meet her. To see what she looked like? Or at least that she'd try to be friendly. How dreadful could an eleven-year-old girl be?

Chapter Fifteen
Meeting Bella

Mum had never been to East Dulwich before so Anthony had told them he would meet them outside the station. The sun had been trying to show its face for the entire journey up from Chichester and finally popped out from behind scurrying clouds into a clear blue sky. As Mum and Willow walked out onto the pavement in front of the station, they could see Anthony checking his phone, sunglasses on, standing with his back to the ticket office.

'Hello,' Mum said as they approached Anthony. 'We got here.'

'Great. Thanks for coming, again.' He kissed her and pecked Willow on the check. 'I know this is all very disruptive for you both.'

Willow shrugged. She was dreading that Bella would look really ill and deathly like Beth had done in *Little Women*.

'How's Bella feeling?' Willow asked, to make sure. 'Is she feeling ill or is she OK?'

113

'Bella's OK at the moment. She's a bit, you know . . . that I kept a secret from all of them.' He smiled as if to change the subject and led them away from the station.

They walked up a road past an old-fashioned ice cream parlour that Willow looked longingly at. 'We can go there on the way back,' Mum promised. They passed a tiny Italian restaurant, a trendy hairdressers, various clothes shops, and a beauty salon.

Willow felt a text vibrate on her phone in her pocket. She pulled it out and looked as they walked. Stella had sent her a picture of the gang waving. 'Good luck!' she had typed underneath. Willow wished she was there right now, just having a normal day out with her friends.

'We're nearly there,' Anthony said.

'Willow, I hope you don't mind, but I'm going to go and get a coffee for an hour or so. I've got a sketchbook and the paper,' Mum announced.

'Oh . . . ' Willow looked crestfallen. 'You're not even going to come in and say hello?'

Her mum cleared her throat, but didn't say anything.

'We have coffee and some cakes that Maria made with Archie yesterday,' Anthony said, trying to persuade her. 'I do understand if you would rather not though . . . '

Willow looked at her mum. 'Please come in, just for

a bit?' she pleaded, nervous about meeting the Jerrard family alone.

'OK, for a bit,' Willow's mum said, throwing an arm around Willow.

Anthony turned into a garden with a low brick wall. It was a tall semi-detached Victorian house with a cute little front garden. Anthony shoved his key in the lock and opened the dark grey front door. 'We're home!' he shouted through the entrance hall to no one in particular, his voice echoing through the house.

Willow stepped over the threshold and into a new world. Anthony's house felt serene, just like the twins' house did.

'We're in here,' a woman's voice called out from somewhere. Willow and her mum followed Anthony through a door and into the kitchen.

'Wow,' they both said in unison under their breaths. The kitchen had a white stone-flagged floor stretching all the way to the glass concertina doors at the end which were folded right back, giving the impression that the kitchen was actually in the beautiful tree-lined garden. Half the kitchen had a completely glass roof and walls, like a transparent box had been airlifted in and plonked on the back of the house. It was stunning.

At a large battered wooden table sat Maria, Archie,

and Bella. Maria got up to greet them. She was wearing a white shirt over tight black jeans, and sparkly flip-flops. She was delicately pretty with thick black hair cut into a sharp bob; she wore bright red lipstick and had a pair of expensive-looking sunglasses perched on her head. She smiled at them.

'Hello, I'm Maria.' She extended her hand to Willow's mum and then to Willow. She shook hands firmly like a woman in control of a situation. 'Sorry I'm a bit sticky; we've been eating cakes. Would you like to sit down and have one?'

Willow looked at the cakes all arranged prettily on a plain glass cake stand in the centre of the table. They looked delicious but her tummy was clamped shut.

'No, thanks,' Willow said. 'Please can I have a drink of water?'

'I'll get it,' said Anthony, bounding over to the huge American fridge in the corner. He pressed a glass into the water fountain in the fridge door and brought it over to her.

'This is Bella and Archie,' Maria said. Archie waved from his seat and Bella gave Willow a forced smile. 'Helen, would you like a coffee? I've just made a fresh pot.'

'Oh, yes, please, that would be lovely.'

'I made the cakes,' Archie piped up.

'No, you didn't,' Bella almost spat at him. 'You just measured what Mum told you to measure and pressed the button.'

'Bella, he did help lots,' Maria said gently. Archie looked crestfallen.

'Can I have one of your cakes, please, Archie?' Willow's mum said, smiling and pulling up two chairs for her and Willow. 'They look totally delicious.'

His face brightened up at once. 'Yes!' He picked one up and gave it to her without a plate.

'Archie! Fingers!' Maria cried. 'Put it on a plate for Helen.'

'It's OK, I don't mind. We don't normally get as far as using a plate at home.'

Out of the corner of her eye Willow noticed Bella watching her. She sat quietly sipping her water and checking out the space, doing everything to avoid looking at Bella. Even from the other side of the table she could feel a really dark mood radiating off her half-sister like a smoky black smog.

What was surprising was that Bella just looked normal, if a little pale with dark circles under her eyes. In the flesh she looked so like her mum; her hair was thick and dark like Maria's but longer, past her collarbone.

She was wearing a denim mini skirt, purple leggings, and a purple Gap T-shirt.

'Where do you guys live?' Maria asked politely, as if she didn't already know, and Willow and her mum were just visitors they knew nothing about.

'In Weston, a small village outside Chichester in the South Downs,' Mum replied.

'I bet it's really pretty,' Maria smiled.

Willow noticed Bella rolling her eyes as Maria said how pretty she thought Weston would be. Willow hated all this fakeness too. She could feel her head beginning to throb and wanted to say something real to stop all the pussyfooting around.

'I was really upset when I found out Mum had lied to me!' Willow blurted out at the table. She could feel her face burning. Everyone just stared at her in amazement. What had she said? Why did she say that? But she'd known that she just had to break the ice and that if someone else had said anything more about cakes, where they lived, or how long the train journey had taken them she would have probably screamed.

Chapter Sixteen
Willow does some snooping

It was Maria who came to her rescue. 'Yes, it must have come as a great shock to find out you had a dad after all these years. It's a real shock to us as well. To know that the children have a sister they knew nothing about.'

'A half-sister,' Bella said quietly.

'Which half of you is the sister then?' Archie asked. 'The top half or the bottom half?'

'Oh, Archie!' Maria said. 'I hope you're joking.'

He nodded but the question was left hanging in the air.

'The top half is the sister half,' Willow said, going along with the joke. 'From here to here,' and she pointed from the top of her head to her waist.

Maria laughed politely.

'Bella, what are your favourite subjects at school?' Willow's mum asked, looking a bit lost.

Bella ignored her.

'Bella, Helen asked you a question,' Anthony said.

She bent down to fiddle with her high-top trainers,

119

pretending not to have heard either Willow's mum or Anthony.

'Bella,' Maria said in a warning tone. 'Helen wants to know what your favourite subjects at school are.'

Bella looked up and stared at Willow's mum in a really bored teenage way. 'Maths and science.'

'I was always useless at those at school. You're not really a fan of them, are you, Willow?' Mum said, trying to bring her into the conversation.

'No, I'm completely rubbish at anything to do with maths and science. It's like it's written in secret code or something. Stella has to help me every week with my homework.'

'Who's Stella?' Maria asked.

'My best friend; she lives next door. She's really good at maths but her twin brother is even better. He's such a geek.'

'What do you like at school, then?' Maria asked Willow.

'I love writing and english. They're what I'm best at.'

'Willow's been asked to enter a national writing competition,' Anthony piped up and ruffled her hair from his place next to her.

Bella stiffened, her face resembling a human stormcloud. Two tiny fiery scarlet pinpricks appeared in the centre of each cheek.

'What sort of thing do you have to write?' Archie asked.

'Anything I want to. I haven't started it yet,' Willow said over-brightly, very conscious that Bella looked as though she was going to explode any second.

'Do you want to come upstairs and see my room? I've got Scalextric up there and a jellybean machine! I built a massive Lego *Star Wars* scene as well to show you. Do you like *Star Wars*?' Archie looked so proud, it was impossible not to say yes.

'Of course, doesn't everyone like *Star Wars*?' Willow said. 'My friend Jarvis is obsessed with *Star Wars*. He even has *Star Wars* pyjamas, but don't tell anyone.'

'So do I!' Archie exclaimed. 'Come on, come and see!' And up he jumped from the table, catching Bella on the head by accident.

'Oi!' she snapped. 'That REALLY hurt!'

'Sorry!'

'Is it OK if I go and see Archie's room?' Willow asked the adults, desperate to escape Bella's impending fury. She was very aware she was supposed to be making friends with Bella as well, but Bella was being so moody she didn't know how to do it.

'By all means,' Anthony said. 'Bella, do you want to go upstairs with them?'

Again Bella ignored Anthony as if he just wasn't there.

'Bella, Daddy was talking to you,' Maria coaxed.

'He was?'

'Yes, he asked if you wanted to go upstairs with Willow and Archie. Maybe you could show Willow your room as well?'

'No thanks. I feel sick,' she spat out, leaving Willow feeling relieved.

'Why don't you chill on the sofa and watch some TV instead, then?' Maria said calmly.

'OK.' Bella got up and walked through a set of white wood and glass doors to the right of the kitchen door and into the lounge. She gave Willow and Mum a mega-fake smile on her way past.

'Come on,' Archie urged. Willow looked at her mum and gave her a wide-eyed look and she gave her a nod— it was their code for *it will be OK*!

As Willow followed Archie up the stairs she could hear Anthony from the kitchen. 'So sorry about Bella's mood. She's been ignoring me since I told her about Willow.' After that there was just murmuring and Willow couldn't hear what they were saying.

'Here's my room,' Archie said as they walked up to a half-landing where there were two doors. 'That's Bella's room next to mine. Upstairs is Dad's office and Mum and Dad's room.' The house seemed enormous to

Willow, who was used to her compact two-bedroomed cottage.

Archie's room was big with a wooden floor covered in train tracks and Lego creations and a floor-to-ceiling window with a tiny balcony outside. His bed was a mass of crumpled *Star Wars* duvet and he had some cuddly bears dressed as stormtroopers sitting on his head-dented pillow. There were white cupboards to the right of the chimney stack and one of the doors was hanging open, revealing a rail of clothes with shoes neatly lined up underneath.

Willow walked over to the window, careful not to crush any Lego bits on the way. The glass cube and the garden were below her and she could see the grown-ups still at the table, drinking coffee. There was a swing and slide in the garden and right at the back, hidden behind a hedge, was a trampoline. 'I like your garden,' Willow said, turning round to look at Archie, who was staring at her.

'Thanks. Do you like my *Star Wars* Lego?' he asked, sitting down on the floor next to the scene he had been talking about.

Willow sat down next to him. 'Oh yes, you did a good job there,' Willow said kindly, not even knowing if he had or not.

'You're nice. Bella said you wouldn't be, but I think

you are.' He smiled innocently at her, not realizing what he had just said.

'Oh, er, thank you,' Willow said. 'You're not so bad yourself.'

'Is Bella going to get better?' he suddenly asked her.

'Er, I hope so,' Willow said, not knowing what he did and didn't know.

'Dad said you might be able to help her.'

'Yes, that's right. We're waiting to hear if I can. The doctors will let us know soon.' Archie seemed happy with that.

They stayed in his room for a while longer. Archie showed Willow all his prize possessions and Willow ate some of his jellybeans, spitting out the chilli-flavoured one and making him laugh. 'I've always wanted a jellybean machine!' Willow said. 'They're really cool.'

Willow started to worry about leaving Mum downstairs on her own for so long, knowing that she hadn't wanted to come inside at all. 'I'm just going to see if my mum is OK,' she said to Archie.

'OK, I'll stay here.'

Willow slipped out of his room onto the landing. She paused outside Bella's door; it was ajar. She pushed it gently open and peered inside. There were two large windows facing her with gauzy white curtains pulled across to shield the view and dark velvet purple curtains at either side of the windows drawn back for daytime. The walls were also purple—Bella liked the colour purple then, like Willow! Her bed was neatly made with a white duvet cover and purple cushions scattered on the pillow at the head of the bed.

Willow stepped in cautiously and looked behind her to see if anyone was coming up the stairs. She knew she really shouldn't snoop, but she was desperate to see what sort of girl Bella was.

On her mirror she had postcards of the latest boy band stuck up. There were pots of glitter nail polish and lip glosses in boxes on her white dressing table. All the sorts of things that Willow had, bar the boy band, which was so last year. It was all about rock guitar music now for Willow.

'What are you doing?' a sharp voice asked from behind her.

Willow whipped round to face Bella, standing in the doorway and looking cross.

'Er, nothing. I guess I was just being nosey,' Willow admitted.

'Well, don't be.' Bella entered the room and sat on the bed. 'I don't want you here.'

'Sorry, I didn't mean to pry. I like your room. My favourite colour is purple as well.'

Bella just stared at her, her mouth in a straight line. 'I don't need your help,' she said.

Willow didn't know what to say. 'Your dad seems to think you do.'

'My dad's a liar,' she snapped, angry tears welling up in her eyes.

'So's my mum,' Willow replied, trying to make her feel better. 'It doesn't mean they're bad people.'

'They must be—they had you, didn't they?' Bella narrowed her eyes at her, squeezing a tear out onto her cheek.

Willow was stunned.

'Well, my Mum is a good person and, as far as I can tell, your dad is too,' she replied eventually. 'They made a huge mistake in not telling anyone the truth. When I found out I was so angry and wanted to run away. I totally understand.'

'You don't understand *anything*. I can't run away, can I?' Bella sounded choked up with emotion. 'And don't think you know my dad. You'll *never* know my dad like I do. He's MY dad. You can't come in here and steal him and pretend you've always known him.'

'I don't want to steal him! I didn't want any of this either!' Willow kept her voice as calm as she could but she could feel anger bubbling up in her tummy.

'Go away, then, if you don't want this,' Bella growled through gritted teeth. 'Go back to the *pretty* village you live in and leave us alone. No one wants you here.'

Willow stared at Bella open-mouthed. She could feel tears in her eyes and didn't want Bella to see them. She turned on her heels and ran out of the room,

'I hope you're not a match!' Bella screamed after her as she fled down the stairs to the front door, flinging it open and running outside into the sunshine. She didn't know where she wanted to go, just that she needed to get out of there. So she ran as fast as she could with the cries of her mum and Anthony ringing in her ears: 'Willow! Willow! Come back!'

Chapter Seventeen
Ice cream soothes all

There were two rickety white metal tables outside the ice cream parlour under the stripy red and white awning that stretched out over the pavement. That's where Willow's mum eventually found Willow, sitting out of the sun. She sat down next to her.

'I thought you might be here,' Mum said. 'Do you want to talk about it?'

'Nope.'

'Do you want an ice cream?'

'Yes, please.'

'Have you had a look at what they've got?'

'No. Can you get me mint choc chip if they have it? If not, just chocolate?'

'Of course. Sprinkles?'

'If you like.'

Mum got up and went inside, parting the old-fashioned ribboned multicoloured plastic curtain.

Willow sat there, decompressing from the events

earlier. She really hadn't expected Bella to be so angry at her. In her head the fantasy Bella was quietly ill, a cat lover, maybe wrapped in a quilt on the sofa reading a book and snuggling a kitten on her lap. She had been overjoyed at the news of a sister because, like Willow, she had always wanted one. That was the airbrushed version in her head. The reality was much harsher and a lot less fluffy. Bella hated her and that was it. Willow had never been hated in her life. She just wasn't used to it. She was too shocked even to cry. She'd just had the overwhelming urge to get out of the house.

Mum came out, bearing an ice cream that was such a showstopper it could have starred in its own ice cream advert. There were two scoops of mint choc chip with rainbow sprinkles, edible glitter, and a chocolate flake. She was also holding a cone with two scoops of strawberry ice cream for herself.

'Thanks, Mum,' Willow sniffled as her mum sat down, putting the mega ice cream in front of her.

'I just need to ring Anthony and tell him you're OK.' Mum quickly made the call, deflecting any attempts for him to come and meet them.

'What do you want to do?' Mum asked.

'Go home.'

'I think Bella wants to apologize to you.'

Willow didn't say anything.

'What did she say?' her mum asked.

'Lots of hideous things. But basically she said she didn't want my help and hoped that I wasn't a match. But it was the way she said it, like she hated me.'

'Oh, Willow. I'm sorry. She doesn't hate you at all. She's just so angry at her dad for lying. And probably angry at the world for the unfairness of being so ill. I know she was incredibly rude, I could see that, but you also have to remember she's got a very serious illness and if they don't get her a bone marrow transplant, she's going to die.'

'I know. I just didn't want to be there, though. I didn't really . . . like her.'

'And no one can blame you for that. She's only eleven and she's going through a lot at the moment, as are you. But you're well and happy. She isn't.'

Willow looked at her mum and sighed. She really didn't want to go back to the house. She felt stupid for running off. It had seemed like a good idea at the time. Willow didn't like causing a scene, but she had got the idea that, if she ran away without seeing anyone, there wouldn't be the embarrassing confrontation in the kitchen, and she knew Mum would come and find her. Also, she'd been scared that she was going to cry in front of them, and she definitely hadn't wanted to do that!

'I feel stupid,' she admitted. And a single tear ran down her face.

'Oh, Willow, come here.' Her mum hugged her close and stroked her hair. 'You are such an amazing girl. Bella will realize how lucky she is to have you as a sister. Today was always going to be weird. And no one thinks you're stupid or silly for running off. I don't. I totally understand, I really do.' She sat back and let Willow finish eating her ice cream.

'So, shall we head back home?' Willow's mum asked, once they'd finished their ice creams. 'We can just walk round the corner and get the next train back up to London Bridge.'

'No. Let's go to their house and say goodbye and then go.'

'Are you sure?' asked Mum.

Willow nodded, feeling that it was going to be mega awkward. She didn't actually want to see Bella again, but she felt as though she needed to show her face to Maria and Anthony after running out of the house.

They walked back to Anthony's house and knocked on the door. He opened it and smiled. 'Thank you for coming back,' he said.

They followed him into the kitchen, where Maria and Bella were sitting at the table. Bella looked as though she had been crying. Archie was on the trampoline in the garden.

'We just went for some ice cream,' Mum said cheerfully.

'Oh, at the end of the road? I love it in there,' Maria said. 'Bella likes it there as well, don't you?' Bella nodded. 'Rum and raisin is my favourite.' Maria smiled.

'Sorry I was rude to you,' Bella said, flicking her eyes up at Willow from her seat at the table. She barely made eye contact before looking back down.

'That's OK,' Willow replied. She didn't know what else to say because she could tell Bella wasn't sorry. Willow didn't think that this would be the end of the hostility from her. The force of Bella's hatred had been so strong earlier that Willow felt it would take more than her donating her bone marrow to win Bella round. Willow was desperate to like Bella, but, right now, she just couldn't. And she was certain that Bella wasn't desperate to like her at all!

'None of this is easy for anyone,' Maria said. 'It's just not an everyday situation, is it?' And she gave a nervous laugh.

'No, it's not,' Willow's mum agreed.

'Would you like to stay for some food?' Maria asked.

'Thank you,' Mum said, 'but we're going to head off

now. I forgot earlier, but we got Bella and Archie these.' She placed two large Cadbury's Easter eggs on the table out of her big leather bag.

'Oh, thank you!' Maria said.

'Thanks,' Bella said rather dully.

Anthony called Archie in from the garden to say goodbye and to say thanks for his Easter egg. Archie was a lot more enthusiastic about his egg than Bella had been.

Anthony showed them to the door after everyone had said goodbye.

'So, I'll ring you in a few days to see how you are,' he said to Willow.

'OK.'

'Listen, Willow, it doesn't matter whether you're a match or not, but I would still like to be in your life, if that's OK with you?'

'Yes,' she replied. Bella was going to LOVE that, she thought.

'And in just over a week we should know whether you *are* a match or not,' Anthony said, hugging her. 'Bye, Willow.' He waved at Helen and shut the door.

Willow breathed a sigh of relief and so did her mum.

'I would never normally say this to you, Willow, but when I get home I'm having a large glass of wine.' Mum squeezed Willow's hand. 'What would you like when you get home?'

'Some more food. I feel like I've hardly eaten the last few days.'

'Good idea. I'm starving too, despite the ice cream starter! Why don't we go to that nice Italian place next to the ice cream shop and have something instead?'

'What if those guys come out and spot us?' Willow asked worriedly.

'I don't think they're going anywhere today, do you? Bella looked wiped when we left.'

'OK, then.' By the time they had made the decision they were almost there. When they sat down inside at a table for four in the window, Mum ordered a large glass of red wine and Willow had a Coke.

They chinked glasses when the drinks arrived. 'Cheers,' they said in unison.

'What a day . . . ' Mum said after her first sip. 'It's not every day that you meet the wife and kids of the father of your child!'

'Mum! You make us sound like we're in one of those awful magazines!'

'We could be!'

'Ugh, no thanks!' Willow started to feel a bit better despite the earlier events. She looked at her mum, who winked at her, and she felt glad she had such a great mum, even if she did live in her own little world sometimes.

Chapter Eighteen
One phone call changes everything

They were holding her down again. The faceless doctor and nurse. Willow was trying to scream but she couldn't get a sound out. The nurse was brandishing a giant needle and waving it in her face. 'We're going to turn you over and take out the bone marrow now. Suck it all out. Like a hoover!' And then she laughed maniacally. The anaesthetic hadn't worked; she could feel everything. Help! Help! Why was no one listening to her? She was paralysed. 'You won't feel a thing,' the doctor grimaced as he sharpened what looked like butchers' knives.

Willow woke up, wrestling with the duvet. Her nightie was soaked with sweat and her hair was plastered to her head. She was shaking with cold and fear. That was the fifth time since her meeting with Bella that she had had a nightmare about the possible operation. It was always the same: the anaesthetic hadn't worked and she couldn't tell the doctor. Willow looked at her clock. It was only five a.m. and too early to get up. Instead she changed her nightie and dabbed at her hair with her bath towel. She was too scared to go back to sleep in case she had the same dream, so she lay there in the breaking dawn, worrying. She hated not knowing what was going to happen. Was she going to have the operation or not? Would Bella ever accept her?

Later on that morning, Willow walked as usual to the bus with the twins. They were all back into the swing of school after the Easter holidays. The twins were chuckling about something they had found on YouTube last night.

'You should have seen the guy's face as the bear woke up and chased him. He looked like he was going to poo his pants!' Stella was almost hyperventilating now and had to stop and hold herself up against a tree to catch her breath, while Jarvis doubled over, laughing so hard that his rucksack fell over his head and all his books went everywhere. It didn't stop his giggles, though.

Willow just looked at them and smiled half-heartedly. 'You two are such opposites, but you have the same stupid sense of humour,' she sighed and shook her head, wishing she could join in. But her heart wasn't in it.

Stella was trying to stop laughing but couldn't, and tears streamed down her cheeks. She eventually pulled herself together.

'Honestly, Willow, it would have cheered you up, I promise,' Stella said, after she'd managed to calm down a bit.

'I doubt it,' Willow said sadly, rubbing her eyes.

'Did you have another dream last night?' Stella enquired as they resumed walking. Jarvis was left behind, jamming his books back in his rucksack.

'Yes, and it was worse than all the other dreams. I could feel the pain in my back . . . ' She shivered at the thought.

'I'm sorry,' Stella said. 'It must have been awful. Well, hopefully you won't have to have the operation, or is that the wrong thing to say?'

Willow shrugged. Was it the wrong thing? She didn't know. But the flip side was that Bella would die if they couldn't find another match. Willow felt trapped, just like she did in her dreams.

'But the more you concentrate on how scary the dreams are, the worse they will get,' Jarvis said, having caught up with them.

'Maybe,' Willow said flatly.

Stella hugged her as they reached the bus stop. 'It probably didn't help that you read that book Anthony gave you. I mean, did he read it? The favourite little sister dies without the older sister being able to save her. Hello? Inappropriate or what?'

'Yes,' Jarvis agreed. 'You were a mess that morning when you stayed up reading it. I had to stop you from accidentally walking in front of a bus outside school!'

'Yeah, thanks. Sorry.' Willow yawned.

'Maybe the dreams will stop when you know whether you're a match or not,' Jarvis suggested. 'At least you'll know where you stand then.'

'Yeah, I hope so,' Willow agreed, not even being able to imagine being a match. Normally, when Willow felt all over the place, writing about it or writing *anything* took her out of it. But her laptop and notebook lay abandoned in her room.

Then, just as soon as the limbo had started to feel like a permanent state, it ended with one phone call. That day at teatime the hall telephone rang. Willow knew it would either be a marketing company trying to sell them double glazing, someone wanting them to donate money to a puppy orphanage in Taiwan, or the hospital.

Mum picked up the phone and started talking. It was someone from the hospital. Willow felt her heart leap in her chest and then jump into her throat where she could feel it tap-dancing, making it hard to breathe normally. It was two weeks to the day she had had the blood test. Surely the phone call could only be about one

139

thing. Willow hummed under her breath so she didn't hear what was being said before Mum had finished the phone call and told her in person.

As she put the phone down, Willow stopped humming and waited expectantly for the news.

'Well, that was Doctor Williams from the hospital.' Mum paused, as if gathering herself to deliver the information. 'It turns out you *are* a match for Bella.'

Even though Willow knew that she had been tested and knew she would find out, she still wasn't prepared for the actual possibility that she could be a match and might have to have the operation to save her sister.

'Oh,' was all she could think of to say.

'You weren't expecting that, were you?' Mum said.

'Nope.'

'To be honest, neither was I.'

'When do I have to have the operation?'

'I don't know. I didn't ask too much. I'm going to ring back later and ask all those questions.'

'What now?' Willow asked in a small voice.

'Well, I guess we have a chat when I ring the doctor back. She said she would be there for another few hours. Then we tell your dad. I would have thought he would want to come and talk to you.'

Willow put her head in her hands. 'I can't believe it.'

'There's no pressure, Willow. Remember that. Anthony won't tell Bella you're a match until you're totally sure you're ready.' Who was she kidding? No pressure! Yeah, right, Willow thought to herself.

Willow spotted Anthony's car in the drive as soon as she walked up to the house after school the next day. She opened the door and could hear voices coming from the kitchen. Anthony was sitting at the kitchen table with her mum and there was a pot of coffee on the go. Mum had got out the chocolate biscuits too. The kitchen even looked clean. It was like a royal visit.

'Hello, Willow. Would you like a cup of tea?' Mum asked, getting up from the table.

'Yes, please.'

'How was school?' Anthony asked, before looking down at his hands and shuffling in his seat awkwardly.

'It was OK.' It felt odd, him sitting at the table as though he belonged there, even though he didn't. Willow pulled up a chair next to her mum's empty one so they were both sitting opposite Anthony like an interview panel. There was silence as Willow tried to think of something to say.

After what felt like an age, Anthony jumped in and started talking. 'I really appreciated the fact that you guys came up to visit Bella the other weekend. So did Maria.' Willow knew that. He had said it a million times when he had rung during in the week.

'Bella didn't.' Before she even knew she had said it, Willow voiced the words that had been buzzing around unspoken in her head.

'I know. She's finding all this very hard. As you are, I'm sure. I know none of this is ideal for anyone involved. Least of all you and Bella.'

Willow just sat there and let him think what to say. She was feeling slightly irritated today. She hated feeling under pressure, and it seemed Anthony was only there to try and force her to donate her bone marrow to someone who hated her. Couldn't he think of anything new to say?

'So I'll meet you guys tomorrow for the meeting with the doctor and psychologist,' Anthony said in an over-jolly manner. 'Would you like to go out for a late lunch afterwards?'

'I don't know,' Willow said. 'Can I see how it goes?' She didn't want to commit to anything.

'Sure. I'll do whatever you want.' He paused then changed the subject. 'How's your piece of writing coming along for the competition?'

'It isn't coming along at all.'

'Oh, why's that?'

'I dunno. I just don't know what to write about.'

'Have you tried writing anything?'

'Yes, but it's all rubbish. I feel as though I have a blank television screen in my head.'

'Ha! You are a writer, coming up with that analogy! Have you tried writing about what you know instead of making stuff up?'

'Sometimes I do that, but I mostly write about stuff in my imagination.'

'Some of the best young writing I've seen has been blogging on the internet. It's very interesting. Kids of all ages do it. Maybe *you* could write a blog. Each entry could be a day in the life of you, Willow, aged thirteen.'

'That's a good idea,' Mum said. 'You could write about the bone marrow transplant. So others could see what it's like to donate.'

'Hmm, yes. But how do I do a blog?'

'Have you got a laptop?' Willow nodded. 'Go and get it for me, would you?'

And Anthony spent the rest of his time setting up a blog for Willow on her laptop 'You can add pictures and all sorts.'

'Stella and Jarvis could help you with all that if you get stuck,' Mum said.

'I suppose ... yeah,' Willow said hesitantly. Anthony had just created the most basic one; now it was up to Willow to make it look more exciting and actually interesting to read.

'What are you going to call it?' Anthony asked.

'Does it have to have a name?' Willow replied.

'All the best ones do,' he said. They all sat there for a minute or two, thinking of what Willow could call her blog. But Willow already had a name. 'My Life: What Happens Next?' Because she had no idea. Perhaps writing it might help ...

Before bed, Willow took her laptop upstairs and put it on her desk. Anthony had explained that blogs were like types of open diaries, where anyone could see your writing, even the queen! It was there, in the ether, just hanging out, waiting for avid readers to get hooked in. But how would they know? 'Link it to your Facebook page,' Anthony had suggested. Willow shook her head.

'I'm just going to write it and see how I feel. Maybe I won't tell anyone.'

'Then you may as well just write a diary on your laptop,' her mum had mused.

'No, I want to do a blog,' Willow had replied. 'I just like the idea of it ... existing, like a book in a library.'

So here she was. Free time, blog all set up, the only

thing for it was to start typing, surely. She typed in the name of the blog at the top of the page and started writing for the first time in weeks.

Chapter Nineteen
Blogging

So I like this blogging idea. Maybe I could write it all in gangsta speak? You know, like this: Hey, hot dawg, how's it going wit da bone marrow shizzle? Yo gonna get a sizzling set of wheels fo being such a mazin donor?

Nah, not sure that is totally appropriate for the tone of this blog, with it being such a serious subject. The blog police might come and arrest me for bad grammar and spelling.

Anyhow, so you've heard all about what's going on with me donating my bone marrow to my long lost sister I never knew I had (I promise I'm not making this up), so you can imagine what a pain in the backside (lame joke) it is that I have this phobia. Why couldn't I have the heebie-jeebies about spiders or snakes or blue M&Ms? Having a major operation, with my back injected with massive blood-sucking needles, (deep breath) is like the worst thing I can imagine happening to me. I know it's nothing compared to what B is going through, so I feel ultra-pathetic complaining, I really do, but I'm honestly terrified. I try to pretend to everyone (and even myself) that I'm OK with it, but really, I don't think I am.

I haven't told you about the mega realistic nightmares yet. They're so bad that I can't properly describe them in case it gives me a panic attack, but they involve giant needles and psycho doctors. I'm so scared that I'm literally pinching myself every ten seconds to keep awake so I don't dream. I have woken up screaming before, but Mum didn't hear me—maybe she was in a wine coma. I had a hideous one yesterday where I actually could feel the needles stabbing me. I thought I was going to die on the operating table. Believe me, you don't want to know what it was like.

I've tried talking to Mum about it all, but she just says things like: 'Have you tried relaxing with music instead of reading before bed? I have some lavender oil I can drop on your pillow if you like?' Even when I was standing next to her in the middle of the night shivering so much I had to climb in bed with her. Lavender oil? Really? How's that going to stop satanic doctors butchering my back with those needles? Mum lives in a world where lavender oil is the cure-all for everything and seems to think the oil will send me off into dreamland. But what if it knocks me out so I can't actually wake up and end up having a heart attack while asleep? I feel like I'm on my own little island where no one can even get to me by boat, not even Stella. It's like I'm shouting from the shore but no one can really hear me. And ironically, the only person who really probably would have the smallest inkling of how weird and scary all this is, is B. But I can't talk to her. She hates me . . .

Willow sat back and looked at what she'd written so far. It was so good to write—it was flowing so easily, unlike when she tried to talk about it to anyone. Anthony had been right—writing about what she knew felt more natural to her. She dived back in, eager to carry on.

I told the twins (my best friends) earlier this morning that I'd found out I was a match.

'So you're actually going to have the operation?' Stella asked, gawking at me like she couldn't believe it either.

'Probably,' I replied.

'Come on, tell us what happened,' Jarvis said. 'You can't just say that and not tell us.'

But I felt too exhausted to go into detail. It was all tumbling around my head on a continuous loop. I was just about to answer when Stella butted in,

'Do you know when the operation will be?'

'Er, a few weeks after B starts her chemo.'

'But when's that?' Jarvis asked.

'When we tell B I'm a match.'

'But when will you do that?' Stella said, probing some more. Now I wished I hadn't told them because I didn't want to think about it.

'When I've seen the psychologist.'

'Why do you need to see a shrink?' Jarvis asked.

'To make sure I'm not crazy. Look, do you mind if we don't talk about it? My head hurts with it all. Sorry.'

'Sure,' Stella said. 'No probs.' And after that we didn't talk about it for the rest of the day, but I couldn't talk about anything else either. And when A turned up after school I just wanted him to go away, because ever since he came into my life, it started to go topsy-turvy. I want my old life back where the scariest thing that would happen would be Mum running out of coffee in the morning and being even more of a lunatic than normal. BUT, having said that, A did set up this blog and it has unlocked my writer's block, so maybe he's good for something . . .

So here's hoping that writing this all out of my head onto the endless space of the internet will empty all thoughts of you-know-what so that I can sleep peacefully tonight without any of Mum's hippy oil. Nightmares not welcome here!

One last thought, and one that's bothering me the most: what happens when B finds out I'm a match? Will she refuse treatment and die anyway because she hates me that much? How can I stop her hating me? I just can't see how this is ever going to work out . . .

Chapter Twenty
Phobia central

So today I'm going to hospital to make sure I still have a brain. I'm not sure I do because sometime in the last week it feels like it exploded leaving me with a limited vocabulary and the feeling of needing to rock slowly in the corner like a proper basket case. I'm worried that Stella won't want to know me any more because my mouth won't translate what's going on inside my head and talking is exhausting. It's like I need to give her a can opener and say, 'Open my head and see what's going on, then you'll know why I've morphed into a knuckle-dragging idiot.' It's easier than explaining. Only Stella and Jarvis know the situation. I don't want to tell anyone at school just yet. And, yes, I know they could read this, but I'm not sure about the twins reading the blog just yet.

As far as today goes, all I know is that we're going to meet the doctor—she'll tell us about my operation (yikes), and then the therapist person will chat to me.

Not sure how a chat with a headshrinker (I know it's called a shrink, but headshrinker feels right for this blog!) is going to help. I mean, how can it? They can't make the needles disappear; they're not a magician, are they? Whatever happens, needles are involved. There's no getting away from it. I'm stuffed. Seriously, the mere thought of what they have to do sends me off . . . Oh, I can't even explain, it's just so terrifying, like the thought of swimming with great white sharks. It feels like my heart will burst and I will die of fright.

I've read all the leaflets the nurse, Claire, gave us. I have to be in a stable mindset to donate or they won't allow it. They don't want you freaking out and changing your mind at the last minute. Because by then it's too late. Once you've signed on the dotted line the person receiving your bone marrow starts their chemo, so there's no going back. Chemo kills all their defences and remaining blood cells, like a clean slate, so their blood has no antibodies that might attack the new bone marrow being given to them to make them better. I have to be completely sure I can go through with the operation without having a meltdown or I could put B's life in danger . . .

'Dr Williams will be with us in a few minutes,' Anthony told Willow, Mum, and Granna, when they arrived at the reception. He winked at Willow, trying to get a smile, but he was out of luck.

'Have you started your blog, Willow?' he asked hopefully.

'Sort of,' she shrugged. 'Not really.' She wanted to keep him at arm's length today.

'It's ever so calm,' said Granna, who had come up for moral support, and most likely to have a nose around. 'I was expecting it to be like one of those hospital dramas.'

'They're always set in emergency rooms, Mum,' Mum said, rolling her eyes. 'It's not like that here.'

'I can see that!'

A woman a bit older than Willow's mum approached them. She was wearing smart black trousers and a red blouse with an embroidered neon blue hummingbird on the pocket. Her red hair was scraped back in a bun and she wore an apron over her clothes.

'Hello, Mr Jerrard. Hello, you must be Willow,' she said and shook Willow's hand before saying hello to Mum and Granna.

'I'm Dr Williams, Bella's consultant. Would you like to come to my office and we can have a chat? Dr Angelico the child psychologist is in there as well.'

Willow stood up and looked at her mum. 'I think you should go on your own, peanut,' Mum said.

'Your mum can come as well if you want,' the doctor said.

'Yes, please,' Willow said gratefully. Willow and her mum followed Dr Williams past reception to her office. A man was sitting on a chair opposite the desk where the doctor sat down. He stood up and shook Willow's hand and then her mum's.

'I'm Dr Angelico, a child psychologist.' He had a kind smile and his black hair was peppered with white flecks. He looked like a kids' TV presenter in his loud Hawaiian shirt and black jeans. But he must have been older than Mum and Anthony.

'Today we're going to make sure that you're happy to go through with the operation,' Dr Williams said, looking Willow squarely in the face as everyone sat back down.

Willow nodded. 'Happy' was the wrong word to use. Willow wasn't happy to do this at all. But the image of Bella dying, just like Beth in *Good Wives*, slapped her in the face . . . The difference was Beth was nice. Bella wasn't. Oh, it was so complicated!

'I have a consent form here for you to sign, Ms Fitzpatrick,' Dr Williams said to Willow's mum. 'I'm just going to go through the details of what will happen before and after the extraction, and then Willow can talk to Dr Angelico about how she's feeling and if she has questions she can ask me or Dr Angelico. There's no pressure here at all. If you're unsure about any of this and want to back out before you sign the consent form, you can. We are here to help.' Dr Williams was very precise and professional and didn't let her personality filter through her words.

'Can I just say something?' Mum asked, before Dr Williams started her information overload.

'Of course.'

'Willow is extremely squeamish, and blood and needles freak her out. She passed out when the nurse took blood last time. Just talking about it can set her mind racing and she's been getting nightmares because of it.'

'OK, that's good to know,' Dr Williams said in a less formal manner. 'I will trot out my gore-free version. And maybe Dr Angelico can chat about the nightmares. They don't sound good.' She smiled at Willow and suddenly became less like a doctor and more like a nice lady you could talk to about anything.

So Dr Williams relayed the facts in a blood-free manner to Willow, and Willow only felt sick for one second when the doctor said they would have to take the bone marrow out of the bones in her pelvis while she lay on her front, just like it had said on the internet.

'Was that OK?' Dr Williams asked. 'I tried really hard to not mention anything that might make you pass out. You looked OK. No fainting yet, though we do need to take blood again after your chat with Dr Angelico. If it's OK with you I'll stay in the room for this initial consultation, but for future ones, you'll see Dr Angelico on your own.'

'That's fine. I think I only passed out last time because I saw the blood coming out,' Willow said hopefully, wishing that there was no need to take blood and she could just leave.

'This is a very kind thing you are doing for your sister,' Dr Angelico said. 'It must be very hard because you dislike needles so much.'

Willow nodded. Calling Bella her sister didn't feel right. She was like a stranger.

'And Dr Williams tells me that you only found out about your father's existence recently, in the last month.'

'Yes, before Easter.'

'That must have been such a shock.' Mum looked a bit hot under the collar at the mention of this.

'How did that make you feel?'

Willow looked at her mum. She felt weird having this conversation with Mum here.

'Er, I was angry.'

'OK. I can imagine that you were. One minute you had no dad and the next minute you had a dad who wanted you to help your sister out. So how did you get from being angry to being here, making the decision to help Bella? Is this something you are really sure about?'

Willow was silent. She felt like a rabbit in headlights. This was the first time since she had begun to feel uncertain about it all that someone had actually asked her outright what she really felt. And this someone was a proper official doctor. Sweat trickled down her sides from her armpits and her palms seemed to have sprung a leak.

'Are you OK, Willow? You look a bit pale,' Dr Angelico asked. He looked at her mum to see what she thought.

'Willow, what's the matter?' Mum coaxed.

'It's the needles, the operation, the thought of it . . . ' Willow finally said rather quietly.

'The thought of what?' Dr Angelico asked.

Willow gathered herself because she hadn't even said this out loud before. She didn't know how to put it because she thought they would think she was ridiculous, especially when thinking about what Bella had to deal with. Willow didn't want to seem as though she didn't care. But she couldn't get past the terror.

'The thought of the operation and the ... the needles ... and going to sleep with a needle in the back of my hand ... What if I have a nightmare and, because of the anaesthetic, I can't wake myself up and I ... die of fright?' And she burst into tears.

'Willow, why didn't you tell me you felt as bad as this?' Mum asked, aghast.

'I tried, but you didn't really listen,' she cried, scared she was going to get into trouble for feeling so weird. Mum hugged her.

'I'm so sorry, peanut. I should have been more supportive.'

'Willow, this is OK,' Dr Angelico soothed. 'All perfectly normal.'

'Poor Willow,' Dr Williams said gently. 'You have been in the wars, haven't you? Just let me put you out of your misery about a few things. If you have the operation and are under general anaesthetic, you won't have any nightmares. One minute you will be awake, the next you will be asleep, and then the next you will be awake again. No time will have passed for you. It will be like that,' and she clicked her fingers. 'And we can use a gas mask instead of a needle to give you the anaesthetic initially. There will be one in your hand when you wake up, but we can tape it over to disguise it.'

'But what if the anaesthetic doesn't work and I can feel it all happening?' Willow sobbed. 'That's what the dreams are about. No one can hear me because I can't speak.' Dr Angelico passed her some tissues and she blew her nose.

'Willow, you obviously have a very real fear going on here,' he sympathized. 'And as it stands, I would say we need to review everything going on in your life because I get the feeling it isn't just the needles. You've had a lot to deal with in the last few weeks.'

Willow cried quietly into her tissues. She wiped her eyes, but they just continued to fill up.

'Yes, at the moment you aren't in any fit state to donate,' Dr Williams said. 'And I agree with Dr Angelico, we need to help you face all the new family issues that have happened and *then* tackle the phobia.'

'But what about Bella?' Willow squeaked out between wiping her eyes and blowing her nose.

No one said anything for what felt like ages. Eventually Dr Williams spoke. 'Bella is stable at the moment . . . '

'I have a cancellation this afternoon if you can wait for a bit? Then we can talk it all over in detail,' Dr

Angelico said to Willow and her mum before Willow could ask any more questions about the state of Bella's health.

'What do you think, peanut? Would you be up for that?' Mum asked.

'Yes, sure,' she answered.

'Willow, I want you to know: no one is angry with you. We understand. An extraction is a huge thing to agree to even when everything in your life is on an even keel,' Dr Williams told her. 'But you have more than enough to deal with at the moment. I will talk to your father and tell him things are on hold for the time being.'

Willow slumped against the back of the chair. She was dreading Anthony finding out. What if he went crazy and was cross with her for delaying it all? What if she never got the go-ahead to donate? And what about Bella? What if the illness got worse? Just because she was stable now didn't mean that it would last for ever. Willow knew Bella was on borrowed time and that she would only remain stable for so long; anything could happen, and Willow didn't want to think what that really meant.

CHAPTER TWENTY-ONE
The headshrinker

The meeting with the doctors was a disaster. And on top of that I had to have another one with the therapist, Dr Angelico.

'Tell me about your meeting with your sister. Dr Williams told me you met her last weekend for the first time.'

I told him everything, even the bit about her screaming at me. I didn't want to paint her in a bad light and it felt like I was doing that, but all I was doing was telling the truth.

'Do you think if B had accepted you and you guys were the best of friends already that you would be having these nightmares?'

'Well, I only started having them after our disastrous meeting. And I knew about the extraction and the needles before that.'

'It's probably compounded all your fears about the

161

operation. It's sometimes easier to do something very difficult when you know you're going to get something out of it. But deep down perhaps you feel like you're not getting anything in return.'

'What do you mean?' His psychobabble was confusing.

'Well, before you met B what did you think?'

What had I thought? That we would be best friends? 'I thought that she would at least try to be nice.'

'So when she was the exact opposite, and you were offering to do something you are frightened of, it probably shocked you, upset you deep inside. It's understandable.'

'Yes, I suppose so.'

'It must feel like she would rather die than let you help her.' I nodded in agreement. 'So your resilience and determination to put your fear of needles to one side in order to help disappeared because what's the point? She hates you and will never want to be your sister, even if you do save her. Thus the fear has overcome you.'

'Maybe. I don't know.' It sounded plausible but knowing the reason didn't make the fear go away.

'You know it's really nothing to do with you. It's possibly to do with her. She's most likely angry at having the illness.'

'Really?' I said hopefully. 'So there could be a chance that she might come round?'

'That's not something I can help with,' he said. 'I wish I could.'

I wish he could too. I know it's wrong, and it's a thought I keep having, but I almost want to shake B and say, 'I want to help you. I want to be your friend. Stop pushing me away. We can get through this together.' Instead we're both going through it separately. And it seems so stupid. We could support each other, like Jo supports Beth in *Little Women* . . . I didn't say any of that, though.

'B will be having her own counselling sessions. Let's hope that they help her.' He looked down at his notebook. 'You said earlier that you felt angry when your father only contacted you because he needed your help. Do you still feel angry now?'

'Yes. And no. He said I mustn't think it would change how he feels about me, when Dr Williams told him I needed some time out, but . . . '

'But what?'

Out of nowhere, when I had been totally fine discussing B and nightmares and all sorts, I was overwhelmed by a surge of emotion. I wanted to get up and run because I could feel the tsunami of tears coming again. What was wrong with me? In real life I HATE crying! I didn't know who I was any more.

'Can you voice it?' Dr Angelico asked me.

'I don't believe him,' I managed to get out.

'You don't believe A means what he says?'

'No. I just think he's saying it so I will calm down and get over my phobia and get the all-clear to donate.' I hiccuped, stifling another sob.

'I don't know A so cannot speak for him. Would it help, do you think, to have a session with him here?'

'No, not yet. I don't think I want that.' I couldn't face hearing what he really thought right now. The thought of family therapy all sitting round in a circle made me cringe.

'And you do want to donate, don't you? I have to ask this so we have something to work towards. I'm not pressurising you in any way.'

Right then, just for a split second, I didn't know. And he knew it. He must have seen it in my eyes.

'I won't judge you, Willow,' he said kindly.

'I want to donate, there's no way I want Bella to die, no way,' I said vehemently. 'But the fear. I can't even tell you. I'm scared the doctors will have to hold me down on the bed to get the mask on . . .'

'Let me assure you right now that would never happen. We wouldn't let you get anywhere near an operating theatre if we all still thought that would happen. You would have to be one hundred per cent positive you could do it and have the fear under control.'

That was a bit of a relief to hear, but also not because it meant I had to get a grip of the phobia and it all felt so out of control in my head. I don't remember it ever being this bad before. But then all I had ever had to face was the odd injection and gory scenes from films which I could avoid watching by covering my eyes. This was real-life gore and it was actually happening to me.

'I feel so guilty,' I said to Dr Angelico. 'It's up to me and I have this stupid fear and I feel so . . . stuck. Bella's depending on me.'

'There's no need for you to feel guilty for having these feelings. I would say it is almost impossible for you to conquer the fear with all this emotional debris in the way. We need to clear the path so you can see where you are going.'

But how long would that take? I don't have years to sort through the emotional baggage has been dumped on me. I want to be cured, never come back here for any more meetings, and just donate so Bella can live. Why can't I just get over it right now?

'Now firstly, let's try some relaxation techniques and visualizations to help you deal with needles and squeamishness.'

So he made me close my eyes and talked me through an injection, making me imagine I was on a seashore, and it was actually quite nice. We did other visualizations too and then at the end he said I should practise it at home, every day.

I didn't have to have blood taken in the end because of my not being able to donate right now. So that was like the only good thing that came out of it all! When it was time to go he walked me out to Mum, and they had a chat and then he said he would be prepared to see me on Monday morning, meaning missing school, again. Today was Friday. I had missed double maths. I'm not even sure if double maths was worse than this. Actually I think maths just about scraped into the lead.

I was feeling very frustrated. I had wanted an instant fix. Everything still felt the same. It was just like the limbo before when I didn't know if I was a match or not for B. Mum went to the loo and said she would meet us downstairs. A had gone but had asked Mum to say goodbye—he had had to take a work phone call. I kind of couldn't believe he had gone without saying goodbye. Mum and Granna had looked all shifty when I had asked where he was. Granna ushered me quickly towards the stairs, and was being all flustered and odd. 'Come on, pet, we have to hurry—the rush hour will be hideous.'

'Why can't we take the lift?' I said.

'Er, because it'll take too long. We'll have walked down by the time one arrives.' As we reached the doors to the stairs opposite the lifts, I heard the doors ping behind me.

'Come on, pet, let's go.' Granna was through the door quicker than lightning.

Something wasn't right. I looked round. The doors slid open and I recognized A first and I was about to call out when my breath caught in my throat. He stepped out of the lift and behind him appeared M and B. They all walked over to the reception desk. Granna had sneaked up behind me.

'Pet, we thought it best you didn't see her in case she puts two and two together and realizes you're a match before the doctors tell her—why else would you be at hospital? She knows you've already been tested. You weren't supposed to be up here so late this afternoon, and B was scheduled for an appointment long after you would have been on your way. It all overran so we wanted to rush out before she arrived. Anthony went downstairs to try and delay her a bit.'

I felt stupid, like I couldn't even be seen. Like I was the poison running though her bones. Just before I turned round to go down the stairs, B looked over and caught me staring at her. Her tired face snapped shut in an instant and she narrowed her eyes at me. I smiled because I actually didn't know what else to do. She pulled her lips into a tight thin line and swiftly turned her back on me. She was never going to come round. It was plain for me to see.

I pushed open the door and took the stairs two a time, my eyes stinging, desperate to get out into the real world and out of the stuffy hospital air.

Chapter Twenty-two
Willow's left out

The next morning Jarvis poked his head through the open French doors. 'Hiya!' he cried, making Willow's mum jump while she sleepily made her coffee, slopping hot water onto the worktop.

'Jarvis! You're bright and cheery today,' Mum yawned. 'Perhaps you can cheer Willow up this morning. I mentioned taking her bowling but she doesn't seem keen. Are you guys around today? Maybe you could come too?'

Willow was sitting at the table, half-heartedly eating toast, and smiled at Jarvis.

'You know me, always partial to a game of bowling.'

'Where's Stella?' asked Willow.

'She's gone to Lola's for the day. Mum's dropping her off now, so I thought I would see what my other twin sister was up to.' He smiled at Willow. 'But you'll see her at the party later.'

'What party?' Willow asked, puzzled.

'Hattie's party. It's her birthday. You're invited.'

'I didn't get an invite,' she said stiffly.

'You will have. I'm sure Stella brought them back after the shopping trip last weekend.'

'I didn't go. I had a meeting with Bella.'

'Oh.' Jarvis smiled and shrugged at the same time. 'Perhaps she forgot to give you yours at school?'

Willow shook her head and tears stung her eyes. Why hadn't anyone told her about the party?

'Don't worry about it. She's invited everyone, even me!'

'You can go,' Mum said, listening in to the conversation. 'We've got no plans. I can drive you all there if you want?'

'It will just be me and Willow because Stella is getting ready at Lola's house and going straight there to help set up.'

'Well, we can go without Stella, can't we?' Mum said, a bit over-cheery. 'Have you told Jarvis about your blog, Willow?'

'Blog? What blog?' Jarvis asked, sounding excited.

Willow inwardly sighed; she didn't want anyone to know about the blog yet.

'About my life and the bone marrow *thing*.' Willow couldn't even bring herself to say donation.

'Can I read it? What's it called?'

Willow shrugged. 'If you want. It's called 'My Life: What Happens Next?'; I haven't written much yet.'

'Oh, that's so cool!' Jarvis cooed.

'Maybe you could show Willow how to jazz it up a bit?' Mum suggested. 'You know, make it more all-singing, all-dancing? It's for the writing competition.'

'Of course. Happy to help. Do you want to do it now?'

'Thanks, maybe later, Java? After bowling?'

But after bowling Willow didn't want to do anything. Jarvis said he would come and knock for her when it was time to go for the party.

'Why don't you text Hattie if it's bothering you?' Mum said to Willow.

'If what's bothering me?' Willow asked.

'If you're, you know, put out that you didn't get an official invite.'

'Mum! I don't care! I don't want to go anyway. I feel . . . too tired.'

'I'm just saying . . . '

Suddenly Willow's phone pinged and, as if she had been earwigging on their conversation, Hattie sent through a hasty apology about the party invite, saying she had meant to give it to Stella, but forgot, then Stella didn't remind her, then they all forgot because no one had seen Willow properly. But did she still want to come to the party? If she wasn't busy.

Willow bit her lip. They forgot . . .

So today got off to a good start. I had a nightmare last night, but managed to wake myself up before the needles attacked me. I hadn't had one since the day before. Good to see the head-shrinking has been so effective . . .

Stella has gone AWOL to Lola's house, the resident Boy Obsessive who can't seem to talk about anything other than what boy she has a crush on and why. I'm not being mean—she would be the first one to admit that—she has a one-track mind. I never thought Stella was like that, though. Surely she will get bored? I don't get it. Also she never even came to see me when she knew I had been to hospital the day before to see the doctors. And I can't believe she forgot to give me Hattie's invite and that they ALL forgot! Hello, I am still here. I know I haven't really been tap-dancing with joy but it would still be nice to be asked. I can't decide whether to go or not. I feel so separate from everyone and everyone's just getting on with their stuff. My life is in a different world right now . . .

I have another meeting with Dr Angelico on

Monday morning. Granna says I have to have a positive mental attitude towards it. And to practise the meditation thingies like the doc said. I do like them but how do they test to see if I'm not freaked any more? I can't lie, can I? Because I still think that the minute they gown me up for theatre I'll be running off in the opposite direction, screaming. And B will be stuck in isolation with no bone marrow and the possibility of dying in there. All the psychobabble help in the world doesn't feel like it could make this work out. PMA, positive mental attitude . . . I tried twice this morning to imagine a needle piercing my skin and drawing blood (yuk, yuk, yuk, that just made my head spin), but I broke out in a cold sweat and thought I could have puked. I. Am. A. Total. Failure.

And A's doing my head in. He won't stop ringing. I don't want to talk to him. He rang four times today before we went bowling. Each time Mum said I was busy, out on my bike, or next door—all lies, of course. I don't know what to say to him. I feel bad enough as it is. How do I know he isn't ringing just to make sure I'm trying my hardest to get over this phobia? It feels like he's stalking me, checking up on me. Not because he wants to talk to me regardless. When he rang the last time I could hear Mum talking to him in the hall.

I poked my head out of my bedroom and earwigged. I wished I hadn't.

'I'm so sorry A. What have the doctors said?'

'Really? Gosh, so there isn't loads of time? Poor Bella. Can they do anything?'

I obviously couldn't hear what he was saying but it wasn't good.

'No, of course I won't tell her. She feels so awful anyway; this will make her feel even worse. Hopefully Dr Angelico can really help her.'

My stomach plummeted to the bottom of my slippers. I didn't need to have bat hearing to work out what was going on. Bella must be getting worse.

'Yes, she's got another appointment Monday. We'll see. Try ringing later.'

I crept back into my room. The biscuits I'd brought up to help me write suddenly lost their appeal.

When he rang an hour later I reluctantly spoke to him.

'How are you keeping? I've missed talking to you.' I didn't want to say the same. Because it wasn't true.

'I've been busy.'

'I'm sure you have. How are the twins?'

'Fine.' The conversation was like a slow kind of drip, drip water torture.

'Would you mind if I came down for a spot of lunch tomorrow? I can take you out. Anywhere you want.'

What was the point? I couldn't face the desperation in his voice and the fact that I was the biggest let-down on the planet. He was probably only keeping up these chit-chats to make sure I pulled myself together. He probably hated me. I mean, I would hate me, if I were him. Imagine thinking you're about to win the race only to find out someone's moved the finish line . . .

'I'm busy tomorrow.'

'For the whole day?' A asked sounding surprised.

'Yes. I've loads of homework.' What a lie!

'Oh. That's a shame. Can I meet you after your appointment on Monday then?'

I wildly tried to think of an excuse. 'I'm going to Hattie's that night. So we have to rush off.'

'Willow, are you avoiding me?'

Silence from me. This was so awkward . . .

'Willow, it's OK if you are. I want you to know you'll always be my daughter. You don't need to hide.'

Daughter. That was the first time he had called me that. I could feel my eyes well up but I blinked any tears away. He was saying all the right things to make sure I stayed on board. Maybe he thought I would change my mind and pull out? Talk about keeping me sweet . . .

'Look, I'm here if you need me, OK? Ring me any time.'

'I'm fine on my own,' I croaked out, wanting to tell him I'd managed for thirteen years so far, but I just couldn't voice it.

'Is there anything I can do?' he asked, sounding pained.

'Leave me alone!'

'Well I—' I did something awful. I pressed the button to end the call. I've never done that to anyone before. But I couldn't carry on the conversation and I didn't know how to end it. I just found it hard to believe that he cared as much as he said he did. Especially when it all looked like it was going belly up and the only reason was because of me. For the millionth time—why can't I just not have a phobia? I need to get out, stop hiding in my room . . .

Chapter Twenty-three
Hattie's party

'Willow's here!' Hattie shrieked as she opened the door. 'Where've you been? Are you OK? You keep sneaking off!' Hattie pulled Willow into a big hug. Stella came bounding over and hugged her too.

'I didn't know you were coming! I thought you were, er, you know, busy . . . ' No one else knew about Willow's predicament or why she was missing school, apart from the headmaster and the twins.

'Jarvis dragged me out.' Willow smiled. It was good to see Stella and the others. They were all there, most of the class and some from the other classes too. The house was heaving and, because it was quite a nice evening, there was overspill into the back garden.

Stella didn't have a chance to ask Willow anything because Lola came up and, after saying hello, grabbed her hand and dragged her off to where the boys were hanging out next to the food.

'Stay there, I'll come back in a minute!' she shouted over her shoulder, giggling as Lola took over.

'Since when did Stella like hanging with *them*?' Willow sniped.

'Since Danny started fancying her.'

'What? When? She never told me!' Willow cried to Jarvis.

'You haven't been here all the time.'

'I only missed a day out of school.'

'That's all it takes. Been brewing for a while. Anyway, your head was somewhere else even when you were here last week.'

'Are they . . . you know . . . Going Out?' Willow asked, trying to sound as though she didn't care.

'No! He's not asked her yet. He just fancies her.'

Willow wouldn't know if a boy ever fancied her or not. Her nose was always in a book. But she knew how it worked from listening to Lola droning on about it. Just because a boy fancied you didn't mean you were Going Out. You had to fancy them back. But did Stella . . . ?

Jarvis must have read her mind. 'I'm not sure whether she fancies him—she wouldn't tell *me*, but Lola, being the expert, is loving it!' Jarvis laughed his head off.

Emma and Hattie came over. 'What about Danny fancying Stella?' Emma cooed. 'Does she fancy him back?'

'I think she might. She said last week that she can't make up her mind whether she does or not,' Hattie replied.

'Did you get lots of cool presents?' Jarvis asked Hattie, trying to change the subject.

'Yes, Mum got me Topshop vouchers,' she smiled, and then her face clouded over. 'I only got a card from my dad. Said he would give me my present when he saw me. But I don't know when that will be.' Hattie suddenly looked as though she was going to cry and Emma grabbed her hand and squeezed it.

'Don't worry. I'll help you spend your Topshop vouchers! You'll come, won't you, Willow? We can have a day out and you can have a trying-on session with all of us,' Emma said to Hattie. 'That might take your mind off your mum and dad and everything, you know . . . '

Willow grabbed Hattie's other hand. 'I'm sorry, Hattie,' Willow said. 'It must be so rubbish.'

'It's OK, Willow. Thanks,' she said, putting on a smile. 'Let's party! I need to dance! Cheesy disco, here we go!'

Hattie ran off to the kitchen where the tunes were with Emma following in her wake.

'Do you want to dance, Willow?' Jarvis asked. 'Let's go and show off our best moves.'

'I'm good, thanks. You knock yourself out.' Willow checked the bus timetable app on her phone. If she legged it now she could get a bus direct to the village green and be home in bed reading in less than an hour. Mum might go mad she got the bus, but she was willing to chance it rather than face a barrage of questions and have to hang around and wait for her to arrive. Knowing Mum, that could take for ever. And she was just so desperate to leave right now. She didn't think anyone would even be bothered . . .

'I'm not leaving you on your own!' Jarvis exclaimed.

'I'm not on my own. There're a million kids here! How can I be on my own?'

'If you're sure . . . ' Willow peeked through the lounge and into the kitchen and could see Emma throwing out an imaginary fishing line and trying to reel them both in. 'Ow, she got me!' Jarvis pretended to get caught and Emma pulled him through the kids in the lounge until he joined her on the dance floor. As soon as he started moving, his goofy mates fell about laughing at his dodgy footwork. Willow took one final look and scooted for the door before anyone really noticed she had even arrived. She ran away from the party and headed to the bus stop. The bus was just pulling up. Willow got on and flashed her pass from her bag. She took a seat and texted Jarvis: *Sorry. Have gone home. Just wasn't in the mood. See you later xxxx*

How can everything change in the blink of an eye? I should've stayed in last night. It was a mistake going to the party. I felt like a ghost, like I was invisible. Not only do I have the Reality Show From Hell family drama going on, but my best friend seems to have changed into someone else entirely. How did I not know Stella had suddenly become interested in boys? Why didn't she tell me? Are we not friends anymore? It kind of stings, you know. I knew something like this would happen because of everything that's going on. I knew Stella would get fed up with me being rubbish. But this? I can't believe it! I feel so stupid. It really does feel like ever since I steamed open that letter (which now seems like a hundred years ago), life has tied itself up in knots. All because of a massive cover up made by two people thirteen years ago. I know that wouldn't have stopped B from getting ill, but at least we would be proper sisters and it wouldn't be such a mess. I wonder if B ever wishes she had always known about me so it wasn't a shock? Or is she stabbing a voodoo doll right now? She must be—my arm's aching . . .

So I was sitting in the garden earlier, trying to read a book to zone out, and Stella came round through our shared garden gate. I pretended to carry on reading for a bit to see what she would do.

'Hey,' she said, when I didn't look up.

'Hey.'

'What you reading?' I held up the front cover. It was *Goodnight Mr Tom*. 'Oh, I love that book!'

It felt awkward. We always knew what to say to each other. Except right this very second.

'Why did you leave the party yesterday?' Stella said, sounding all hurt, which made me kind of cross. 'I didn't even get a chance to talk to you about the hospital.'

'You ran off with Lola to hang out with Danny and that lot,' I spat out, probably a bit too scathingly.

'But I wanted to see you too. I haven't seen you properly for ages apart from at school. And you haven't been texting like normal.'

'You haven't texted either. I've been here. You went out yesterday with Lola.'

'I didn't know you were here. I thought you were meeting A.'

'Not this week, no.' I didn't elaborate, allowing the chasm of awkwardness to widen between us.

'Are you in a mood with me?' Stella asked carefully. 'Is that why you left the party?'

'When were you going to tell me you liked Danny?' I said quietly.

'I don't!'

'Well, whatever it is.'

'It isn't anything.'

'If it isn't anything then why were you running off at the party to hang out?'

'I didn't. Lola made me and I was just going to come back and see you, but you'd gone.'

I sat there fuming and had no idea why. Normally this wouldn't be a big deal. We would laugh about Danny fancying Stella and see what happened. I didn't know what it was about. I just knew I didn't like feeling so awful.

'I'm going. You obviously are in a mood with me. I don't know what I've done. Hope you enjoy the book.' And before I could say anything, Stella turned on her heels and walked swiftly through the gate and back to her house.

I sat there open-mouthed. What had just happened? Had we just had an argument? Had Stella just walked off in a huff? Mum came out of her shed at that exact moment.

'Where's Stella?'

I found myself on the verge of tears again and unable to speak. This was becoming a habit and something I HATED.

'What is it, Willow? Have you two had a fight?' I shook my head and got up from the deckchair and ran into the house, upstairs to my room and started blogging.

I don't fit in my life any more. It isn't my life; it's someone else's life. The only place I feel normal is when I'm writing. So I'm going to write and write and write until there's nothing else to write about!

Chapter Twenty-four
Stella breaks the stalemate

After her run-in with Stella, Willow checked her phone and there were no texts. Should she send a sorry text? She didn't know. But what was she sorry for? What if Stella just ignored her? What if she'd gone over to see Lola or Hattie without her, again? Willow's mind was so full of what-ifs she didn't hear the first knock on her door. The second one was louder. 'Can I come in?'

It was Stella.

'Yes,' Willow said, feeling a bit wary.

Stella pushed open the door. Willow sat on her bed, unmoving.

'I read your blog.'

'Oh.' Willow wasn't expecting her to say that. That hadn't been on the what-if list!

'Jarvis told me about it. He'd read it and said I should take a look.'

'I hadn't really meant anyone to read it yet . . . ' She

hoped no one else had; she really should go back and make sure it wasn't too . . . honest.

'It's great! I whizzed through it.' Willow smiled to herself. 'Willow, I had no idea you were in such a mess about everything. I'm so, so sorry I've been off doing other things. I should have come straight round on Saturday, but I really did think you were doing new family stuff. And I thought you needed to be on your own.'

'They aren't my family!' Willow protested.

'Sorry, I meant meeting Anthony or Bella or the doctors.' Stella paused. 'I didn't realize the dreams were as bad as that and that you've been told you can't donate yet. You haven't been talking to me so I didn't have a clue.'

Willow shrugged.

'Are you really not going to be able do it?' Willow shrugged again, scared to say anything.

'But you're a match . . . And Bella's getting worse.'

'I know!' And Willow burst into tears.

Stella rushed over from the door and sat next to her friend with her arm around her.

'I feel such a mess. I don't want to be the reason Bella . . . dies. I don't know how much worse she is or how long she's got . . . I'm not supposed to know.'

'I can't imagine how hard it is. It's like you need someone to wave a magic wand over you to stop the phobia. It's a pity Dr Angelico can't do it!'

'You really did read all the blog, didn't you?' Willow laughed through her tears.

'Of course I did; it's addictive! I liked the grumpy part about me and Danny. Ha ha.'

'I must go back and change stuff,' Willow muttered.

'No! That's why it's so good. Because it's real! Don't change it, ever!'

'OK!'

Stella remained with her arm around Willow for a moment, not saying anything. Finally she spoke: 'Maybe forget about Bella for a moment, and Anthony. Imagine Bella is me. Would you be able to do this for me if I was dying? Without running screaming from the operating theatre.'

'Of course!' Willow exclaimed. 'I would just man up and use the visualizations to get through it somehow. I wouldn't have a choice.'

'So just imagine Bella is me and all the other family stuff doesn't exist.'

Willow went really quiet for a moment and processed what Stella had just suggested. 'That's a really good idea!' she said eventually and looked at Stella as though she had just told her she had won a holiday to paradise, flying on a private jet with free chocolate for a year thrown in. 'When you put it like that, it makes perfect sense.'

Willow sat jigging her leg as she waited for Dr Angelico to see her on Monday morning. She wanted to run in there and shout, 'Stab me with a needle! Go on, do it!' but thought that would make them call for the men in white coats and a spell in a padded room.

When she had told Mum yesterday evening about how Stella had helped her see things a different way she had been very cautious.

'Peanut, I think that's amazing that you think like that and that you feel you can do it. But it's going to take a lot more than that to convince the doctors. I mean, you were a gibbering wreck on Friday and you've already fainted once. They're going to need to see you can commit to this operation. Everything is riding on it.'

'I thought you'd be more positive than that,' Willow moaned, knowing really Mum was right.

'I am pleased, you know I am. But this isn't just about you, is it? Someone else's life depends on the right decision being made.'

'Willow, Helen.' Dr Angelico appeared by their sides, wearing an even more outlandish shirt than the week before. 'How was your weekend?'

'Good,' Willow replied, desperate to get in the office and prove herself. She could feel adrenaline pumping through her as she held on to her newfound solution.

Willow followed him to his office and sat down.

'So, you look different. Has something happened?'

'Yes! I think I've conquered my fear.'

'I see. Tell me what happened.'

So she told him everything about Stella and what she'd said and how it was like some sort of revelation. She even mentioned the part where she overheard Mum talking to Anthony about Bella getting worse. However, the minute she'd said it she realized that she probably should have left that part out . . .

'So, you suspect Bella is in even more need of your help now? That time may be running out?' Willow didn't like the way he was saying it.

'Yes.'

'So the pressure on you to "perform" is even greater, wouldn't you say?'

'What do you mean?'

'Well, in your head you haven't any time, so you're thinking you'd better get on with it and donate, putting yourself under pressure which could be dangerous in the long run if the fear is still so disabling. And there're all the feelings about Bella and Anthony to contend with . . . '

'No—because, even when I knew Bella was getting worse, I still felt I couldn't do it without freaking out. It wasn't until I spoke to Stella that things changed. As for all the other stuff, it's more important that Bella gets better than if she hates me or if Anthony really wants to be my dad, isn't it?'

'OK. So imagining if Stella were in Bella's situation has wiped the fear completely?'

'No, the thought is still gross, and I feel . . . scared. But I think if I can imagine it differently and really practise my visualizations, I can cope, and get through it without a major freak-out.'

Dr Angelico pressed both hands together into a pyramid shape and gave a massive sigh. 'I think we need to see Dr Williams . . . '

After that first meeting, Willow had to have another meeting with Dr Williams and say all the same stuff to her while she did all the sincere doubtful nodding too. Then they went off and had another meeting on their own while Mum and Willow went to get tea and cake in the canteen. Then they had to go back in for yet *another* group meeting with another psychologist (she was very serious and Willow imagined she would have had her hooked up to a lie-detector machine if they'd had one).

'So,' Dr Griffiths, the other psychologist, said, 'let's say you're OK to donate. We would still need to take that blood sample we didn't take on Friday because you were so distressed. Would you be able to do that now instead? There will be a full medical after this too, though not today. We have to make sure you're emotionally stable first to donate.'

Willow's armpits pricked immediately and started to sweat. Her mouth suddenly felt like a dry bath towel and all she could do was nod because her throat felt as though it would crack.

'Willow, you have to actually say yes,' Dr Angelico said gently to her, 'if you want to go ahead with this blood test.'

'Yes,' she croaked. 'I'll do the blood test.'

'Are you sure?' Dr Williams asked. 'We can do it with you lying down so it makes it easier?'

'That would be good, yes,' she smiled weakly.

So five minutes later they were all in a room with a doctor's couch up against a wall, and Willow was lying down on it, staring at the ceiling. Her mum was holding her feet which were now like blocks of ice, though she was sweating loads.

'Remember what we talked about,' Dr Angelico said. 'Close your eyes, you're on the beach or wherever you want to be . . .' And he talked to Willow to get her going and then let her go; she was on her own with her thoughts . . .

She could feel Dr Williams prodding her arm to find where to put the needle, but, like Dr Angelico told her, Willow visualized something else. Stella popped into her head while she was on the beach. She grabbed Willow's hand and took her to the water, which was the kind of blue that only exists in TV adverts. Willow could almost feel it tickling her toes. She wanted to go swimming . . .

'All done!' Dr Williams announced.

'Can I open my eyes?' she asked, in case there was a vial of blood being waved underneath her nose.

'Yes, the coast is clear!' Dr Angelico laughed.

Willow looked at him smiling at her.

'Well done, peanut!' Mum came over and kissed her. 'You did it!'

'What an achievement, Willow!' Dr Williams said, sounding pleased. 'That's a huge leap forward!'

'So can I donate now?' All three doctors looked at each other. Willow sat up carefully and swung her legs over the edge of the couch. She wasn't even slightly dizzy. The sweat was still trickling down her sides and she did feel a bit funny, but nothing compared to the other times.

'We need to do a risk assessment, Willow. We'll be in touch tomorrow. But I'm very impressed with how you are dealing with this, and with everything,' Dr Williams said. 'For now, please keep this to yourselves until we have made a decision on your emotional stability.'

Chapter Twenty-Five
Emergency calls only

On Tuesday morning, as she was brushing her teeth, Willow heard the doorbell go. When she had finished and come downstairs there was a surprise waiting for her. Next to her school bag on the floor in the hall was a massive cardboard box.

'What's this?' she asked her mum, who was looking on from the kitchen table.

'It's for you.'

'Who from?'

'I don't know. It doesn't say. A courier dropped it off.'

Willow picked it up and carried it to the table so she could open it. She grabbed the scissors from one of the drawers next to the oven and started slicing through the parcel tape. When she ripped off the top of the box loads of polystyrene padding beans shot out like confetti from a cannon. Willow dived into the sea of white and extracted a bright red jellybean machine, an envelope

194

with her name written in familiar black spidery writing taped to it. She opened it and inside was a card with a picture of a teddy holding a placard saying sorry. It was from Anthony.

Dear Willow

I am so sorry you are feeling so upset by everything. The last thing I wanted was for you to feel like this. I guess I have been caught up in how Bella has been feeling and could see you were handling it all brilliantly like a real trouper, so stupidly assumed all was OK. I had no idea your needle phobia was so debilitating, or that everything was just getting too much for you. I naively thought we could be friends easily and that you would accept me as your father eventually one day in the future when all this was over. I can see I have a long way to go before you will even consider me a friend, let alone a father. So to take the pressure off you completely we have decided to find another donor. I should never have asked you. But deep down it was the perfect excuse for me to get in touch and finally meet you. I know it sounds contrived now, but I have wanted to meet you since you were born. And I will wait for you to get in touch when you are ready. I would like us to be friends. I don't want to let you go again, but I realize I must if you are to be happy and come to a decision by yourself of whether I am welcome in your life.

I am very proud of you: of the way you have turned out, of your brilliant writing talent in your blog (yes, I have read it!), and your empathy and kindness. I miss not talking to you and I hope one day we will be able to chat again. You will always be my daughter, and I will always love you. I am sorry it has taken me this long to tell you.

Anthony xx

P.S. Archie chose the present. I hope you like it!

Willow didn't know what to say. It made her eyes sting. She handed the card to Mum who read it silently.

'Mum! What if they've told Bella I'm not a match already? They don't know about yesterday. Can't we ring Anthony and tell him I'm OK to donate?' Willow was in a panic.

'Willow, calm down. You heard the doctors; we can't tell anyone anything until they let us know.'

'Can't you ring the hospital and find out now? They might not ring for hours and hours and it might be too late. They'll tell Bella, surely. She must have guessed something's going on when she saw me at the hospital.'

'Willow, you have to leave for school in a few minutes. This can wait till you get home.'

'Mum, it can't! I know about Bella getting worse. What if this makes her give up hope and she has a panic attack and it messes her up? Even if she does hate me, she might have been counting on it working out?'

'Oh, Willow, you and your overactive imagination,' her mum sighed, but looked startled enough to do something. 'OK, I'll try the hospital.' Mum ferreted about in her handbag and drew out the card with the number on it. She rang it. Willow couldn't bear it so went and found her jacket and shoes and got herself ready while Mum had a brief chat.

'And?' Willow asked, when she came back in the kitchen and Mum had stopped talking on her mobile.

'Dr Williams is in a meeting. The receptionist said that she would ring us as soon as she was out.'

'What about Dr Angelico?'

'He was with a patient.'

Willow felt deflated. She sat down at the table in her jacket and put her head in her hands.

'What are you doing?'

'Waiting until they call.'

'They might be hours, peanut. You've missed a lot of school already and, if you donate, will miss a load more.'

'So what's one more day?'

'Listen, how about we wait here till the last minute and I'll run you to school?'

The twins knocked and Mum told them she was bringing Willow in later. Both of them sat watching the clock, Willow drinking tea and Helen sipping her coffee. The phone remained silent.

'Come on, we have to go. I've got my phone with me if they ring,' Mum said.

Willow dragged herself up to standing and they made their way to the car.

Willow stared unseeing out of the window all the way to school. As they pulled up outside, Mum's phone sprang into life. It was the hospital.

'They want to speak to you.' She offered Willow the phone.

'Willow, it's Dr Williams. It's good news. We're all in agreement that you're ready to donate.' Willow smiled. 'But we need you to agree to regular one-to-one sessions with Dr Angelico via Skype in order to keep you on the right track and on top of your phobia. Does that sound OK?'

'Yes.'

'Have you got any questions?'

'Can I tell Anthony myself?'

'Yes, of course! I'll be in touch later on today with details of what happens next. Well done, Willow!'

Willow was beaming from ear to ear.

'Oh, peanut, great news! Ring him now before you go into school.'

So she rang from her mum's phone. It went straight to voicemail. 'Do you have his landline number, Mum?' she asked anxiously.

'At home, not in my phone—sorry! I can ring him when I get home?'

'No, I need to tell him,' Willow said, desperate to make up for cutting him off the other day. Especially after his lovely letter.

'Then text him your number and get him to call when he switches his phone on. You can always ring him back at break, can't you? Sneakily?'

Willow sat in registration, tapping her foot impatiently on the floor till Stella had to hit her to make her stop. Phones weren't allowed in class, though everyone had them; they just had to be kept hidden in bags. Stella had given Willow a massive hug when she'd told her what the hospital had said.

Just as Mrs Bannister was winding up the roll call, Willow's phone went off. She almost choked. She had forgotten to switch it to vibrate. She had hidden it on her lap under the desk—a major crime by school rules. She silenced it immediately. Stella coughed to try to cover it up, but it was too late.

'Whose phone was that? You know the rules.' Willow stayed silent, hoping that Mrs B would let it go as a mistake. But she couldn't quite reach down into her bag to slip it back in and cover up the evidence. Her hands were shaking so much that she dropped it and it crashed onto the floor by her feet.

'Willow, is that your phone?'

'Yes.'

'Bring it up here, please.'

'But she needs it, Mrs Bannister.' Stella was speaking.

'Stella, I wouldn't butt in if I were you. Willow can have the phone back at the end of the day. I have to say, I am surprised at you, Willow,' said Mrs Bannister, looking very disappointed.

'But it's a matter of life and death,' Stella continued.

'Stella!' Willow gasped. 'It's OK, I'll hand it in.' And she scraped back her chair and got up.

'I'm intrigued,' Mrs Bannister said. 'I've never had a life-or-death situation in my class before.'

The whole class was goggling at perfect Willow getting into trouble. It was like a game of tennis, heads swivelling to see Mrs Bannister and then turning back to see what Willow was saying or doing. Willow looked at her phone when she picked it up off the floor and saw a missed call from Anthony.

She handed it to Mrs Bannister. It started ringing again, this time silently vibrating as Mrs Bannister took it from her. Willow wanted the ground to open up and swallow her whole. Her teacher turned the phone around and looked at the screen.

'Someone wants to get hold of you very badly. Don't they know you're in school?'

'Yes.'

'What's so important it can't wait till after school?' The class collectively held its breath. You could have heard a pin drop.

'Nothing. It's OK.'

'It's not nothing!' Stella burst out. 'Tell Mrs Bannister!' Stella urged. 'Go on, before it's too late!' Jarvis, who was sitting behind her, shook his head in amazement.

'No!' Willow said and turned and started walking back to her desk.

'But she'll find out anyway when she reads your blog for the writing competition!'

'What blog, Willow? What's going on?'

'Stella!' Willow gasped, giving her a warning look. But it was a bit like shutting the stable door after the horse had bolted. She couldn't take the words back now.

The class started whispering to each other. Willow could hear Hattie and Sadie asking if the other knew about a blog. Willow sat back down next to Stella.

'Willow, I think I need to see you before you go to maths,' said Mrs Bannister. And as if to speed things up, the bell rang, signalling the end of registration and the start of lessons.

'Thanks a lot, Stella,' said Willow.

'I'm sorry. But now you can tell her and hopefully she'll let you use your phone!'

'And now everyone will know.'

'But they would anyway. You're writing a blog, doughnut. It's public knowledge. If you didn't want anyone to know, why write it?'

Willow didn't have an answer. She grabbed her coat from the back of her chair and waited for the class to file out before she walked up to the desk.

'So, Willow. Are you going to enlighten me?'

Willow didn't know where to begin. 'Is this to do with the days off you've had lately? The headmaster had OKed them for you.'

'Yes. It's my half-sister. She's poorly.'

'You don't have a half-sister, as far as I know.'

'I do now . . . ' and she let Mrs Bannister in on her family secret. As she told her, Mrs Bannister's face drained of colour.

'So your father, er, Anthony, has no idea you're able to donate?'

'No.'

Mrs Bannister picked up the phone from the desk and handed it to Willow. 'Call him, now! I'll wait outside. Hurry!' And she got up and walked through the door, closing it behind her.

Willow stared at the phone. Her stomach felt as though it was a sea of knots and rollercoaster tracks all intermingled into one big dipper. She pressed the number.

'Hello?'

'Anthony, it's Willow.'

'Ah, hello there. How are you? I rang you back twice but then realized you would be at school.'

'I'm good, thanks. Have you told Bella yet, that I'm not a match?'

'No. I am working my way round to that today. I'm at work just now.'

'Don't tell her.'

'What?'

'Don't tell her I'm not a match. Dr Williams has said I'm OK to donate.'

'I don't understand. The doctor said your phobia is debilitating and you would need a lot of help to get round it.'

'I found a way to get through it, and proved it to them!'

'Is this because of the present and the letter? That wasn't a bribe to make you put pressure on yourself. I meant what I said. You don't have to donate to be my daughter. You are anyway.'

'Anthony, I worked it all out *before* the letter. On Sunday night I had a big chat with Stella and she helped me see a different way of looking at it all. Please—'

The phone went silent. 'Anthony? Are you there?' Still silence. She could hear a class outside waiting to come in for english with Mrs Bannister. The teacher was telling them to quieten down. 'Anthony!'

'I'm here,' he croaked. 'Sorry. I don't know what to say. You took me by surprise. Are you sure, Willow? Because we have to tell Bella today so she can start chemo right away. You have to be concrete sure.'

'I'm sure. Tell her. I'm concrete sure I can do this, I promise.'

'Oh, Willow. You are the best. You were before, but

this is the icing on the cake. Thank you so much. Thank you for this second chance.'

'That's OK. I have to go, I'm at school.'

'Yes, of course. I'll ring you later to sort stuff out and come and see you.'

'OK, bye.'

'Bye. I love you, Willow.'

Willow switched the phone off completely and stood in the empty classroom for a minute before she went outside, letting the conversation sink into her bones. She was surprised. She didn't cringe when Anthony said those three words. Instead she felt a warm glow eradicate all the knots in her stomach. She felt properly calm for the first time in weeks.

Chapter Twenty-six
Good luck, Willow!

It was almost two weeks since the episode in the classroom. Willow was working through some creative writing in english, the last period of the day, when there was a knock on the classroom door. It was Mrs Villier from the school office.

'Can Willow come and see Mr Blake, please?'

'Oh, Willow. What have you done now?' Mrs Bannister laughed. Mr Blake was the headmaster and you only ever got called to see him if you were in massive trouble.

Willow got up, her head full of all sorts of scenarios, the worst one being that Bella had died before they had even managed to save her and Mr Blake had to break the tragic news to her at school.

Mrs Villier escorted her to the head's office at the front of the school. 'In you go . . . '

Willow knocked and pushed the door when she heard his voice say 'Enter'.

'Ah, Willow. Sit down.'

Uh-oh, this is going to be bad, Willow thought, though, as she sat down, she noticed he didn't look cross or upset.

'I just wanted to say good luck for tomorrow and to say how proud we all are of you doing this for your half-sister.'

Willow was so taken aback she just gawped at him. 'Thank you . . . sir.'

'Yes, this must be a hard thing for you to do, what with your needle phobia and everything.' Willow was shocked. How did he know? 'I have been enjoying your blog immensely.' And he looked as though he was trying to suppress a smile.

Willow could feel her face grow red and quickly did a mental recap on her blog to try and remember if she had made any derogatory comments about the head. She didn't think she had, but it was too late now anyway. Oops!

The cat was well and truly out of the bag about the blog. Since Stella had practically advertised it to the entire class, the school had gradually cottoned on to it. People pointed her out and asked her questions. The main thing that people wanted to know was who her secret family was. She had kept their real identities from everyone. Of course, Stella loved the attention, being a star of the blog, along with Jarvis. 'I'll have to get my own agent soon!' she joked to Willow. And it was thanks to Stella and Jarvis that the blog now looked so edgy and cool. Anyone would want to read it even if they didn't have a clue what it was about.

'Talk about teen magazine!' Mum had cooed when she saw the finished design. 'Stella should become a designer when she's older. Your blog looks so urban chic.' Willow rolled her eyes. Urban chic? They lived in the middle of nowhere! More like urban sheep . . .

After her chat with the headmaster, Willow headed back for the last half hour of english before home time. She opened the classroom door and was smacked in the face by the entire class screaming, 'Surprise!' Across the back of the classroom was a banner of stapled-together letters on A4 paper, saying, 'Good Luck, Willow!' There were red and white balloons hanging up on the bookcases and on Mrs Bannister's desk was a huge white cake with 'Good Luck Willow' piped across the top in pink icing. Bottles of lemonade, mini sausage rolls, bowls of crisps, and various other party foods littered the space left on the desk surrounding the cake.

'We had to give you a proper send-off!' Mrs Bannister laughed.

'Oh, wow! Thank you!' Willow was blown away.

'Come and cut your cake!' Stella said. Everyone crowded round while she did it. 'Make a wish!'. Willow wished that the operation was a success. But most of all she wished that Bella would get well again.

And so the last half an hour of school was spent in party mode with everyone asking questions, wishing her luck, and eating the cake that Mrs Bannister had made herself. Stella had made a huge card and everyone had signed it.

Willow lay in bed that night with thoughts buzzing around her head. Tomorrow she was being admitted to hospital. She needed to sleep without nightmares and had only had one since Dr Angelico showed her how to help herself. Remembering what he'd said about not focusing on what she didn't want and focusing on what she did want, Willow imagined a desert island, turquoise sea, palm trees, and dolphins and drifted off eventually, her toes tickled by the lapping waves on the sand.

The next day Willow didn't have time to be scared or nervous because Mum had arranged a major surprise for her.

'Ta da!' Stella and Jarvis jumped out from behind a train timetable while Willow was waiting for Mum to get her ticket.

'What are you guys doing here?' Willow screeched.

'We're escorting you to hospital.'

'No way! How come?'

'Your mum arranged it for us. And we get a day off school—result!' Jarvis said, laughing.

Granna was with them too, so it was quite a party going up to London on the train. By the time they had checked in and settled Willow into her bed it was after lunchtime. There was a girl opposite Willow who was having chemo and just had her mum with her. So Willow's floor show was a bit OTT.

'Let's go round and see Bella,' Mum said, after they had had some late lunch from the canteen and the twins had had a quick nose. 'She's in isolation now, so we can't go in. But you could just show your face so she knows you're here.'

Willow nodded. Her nerves had been kept in check by the twins, but she didn't want to see Bella and this kick-started the wave of jitters in her tummy. She hadn't seen her since the awkward meeting by the lifts weeks ago. Anthony had said they had shaved all her hair off yesterday and that her eyebrows and eyelashes might start to fall out soon.

'The twins can stay here with Granna,' Mum decided. Everyone was congregating on and around

Willow's bed. 'She won't want to be gawped at like an animal in a zoo.'

A nurse took Willow and her mum to Bella's room and buzzed on the intercom. Your sister's here to see you,' she said through the speaker and into the isolation unit. Through the large window next to the buzzer, Willow could see Bella look up from her bed where she was lying. No one was with her and she was watching TV. Wearing a grey tracksuit, she looked so tiny and pale with her head shaved. It was quite a shock for Willow. The room was smaller than the four-bed ward Willow was in. There was a baby-blue sofa with its back to the huge window which stretched to the ceiling, and behind the hospital bed there was a cool psychedelic patterned wall with pink shelves, on which Bella had placed her cards and cuddly toys. The TV she was watching was mounted on the neon-yellow wall opposite, next to a closed wooden door. Willow wondered what was behind it.

'She's not my—' and then the nurse took her hand off the button, not really paying attention and said goodbye. Willow and Mum saw Bella mouth the word 'sister' with a look of blackness on her face.

Mum put her hand on Willow's back and stroked it. Willow could feel hot tears prick her eyes and didn't know what to say after that, but still pressed the button.

'I didn't tell her to say that.' Bella remained tight-lipped. The nurse shouldn't have said that, but, even so, it wasn't very nice to hear her so fiercely reject the word 'sister'.

'I'm sorry you had to shave your hair,' Willow ventured. 'That must have been really hard.' But Bella had turned back to looking at the TV and ignored them both.

Just then the door by the TV opened and Maria came out; Willow could see it was a bathroom. Maria noticed them, waved and then made a motion to say stay there and kissed Bella on the head. She grabbed her coat and joined them in the corridor.

'Hi guys. So tomorrow's the big day?' Maria had written to Willow after she had finally passed the psych test, thanking her again and letting her know how much it meant to her. She had said the doors to their home were always open to her, whenever. It had made Willow feel a bit more upbeat about Bella. Surely she couldn't hold onto the hate for ever if the rest of her family were so accepting?

The afternoon passed in a blur. Maria came by and then so did Anthony who was utterly charmed by the twins. When he was leaving he said, 'How about I take all three of you out for lunch somewhere after this is over? My treat.'

'Is that so we can vet you to make sure you're going to get Willow a pony?' Stella said cheekily.

Anthony almost choked and then burst out laughing. 'If that's what she wants then I will do my best!'

Everyone's gone now. It's just me and Mum. The twins gave me some Lindor chocolates, my total fave in the entire world. I can't eat them until after the op, so I had to hide them from view so I didn't get a craving. When it was time for the twins to go they each gave me a huge hug, and it was then that I realized something. I've been wasting so much time wanting B to accept me as her sister, that I didn't realize that I had a brother and a sister living right next door the whole time. I wanted to run and grab them and tell them thank you for always being there, but hopefully they'll read this and see it for themselves . . .

Chapter Twenty-seven
There's no place like home

As Willow sat up in bed with the starched covers pulled up to her waist, she tried to imagine what it must be like to be Bella instead of her. It was the morning of her operation and she hadn't eaten since last night but there was no way she was hungry now. Her laptop lay on top of the blankets and Willow had been writing from before lights-on earlier. Her nerves had got the better of her and had woken her up very early. Mum was crumpled in a heap on the pull-down bed next to Willow's hospital bed. The lights had come on half an hour ago, but Mum had come prepared with an eye mask and earplugs, so she was still dead to the world. Lizzy, the girl opposite, was still asleep too, but her mum was in the bathroom, brushing her teeth.

Willow tried hard to think how it would feel if she suddenly found out her mum had had a baby before her, someone she knew nothing about; someone who just turned up on her doorstep. Someone who was good at art, looked just like her mum, and captivated her totally. How would that make her feel? she wondered. She didn't know. Because she couldn't imagine what it must feel like to be so terribly ill at the same time. So she tried to do that as well, drinking in her surroundings, her feelings of uncertainty about the operation, her fears of blood and needles, the scariness of the situation. She felt as though she might have a *small* idea of how that felt. Then she topped it off with her secret sibling who was full of the joys of spring and healthy too. How annoying! Willow thought. I bet Bella finds me so irritating she wants to punch me. And then she has to be grateful when all she can think about is whether I'm going to muscle in and take over, push her aside, and be the queen bee. Oh! Willow wanted Bella to know there was no way she was going to do any of those things. But she felt maybe now wasn't the time to do that. And how would she do it? Bella wouldn't listen to her . . .

'Morning!' The nurse breezed in, interrupting Willow's ideas and blogging. 'So you'll be going down in just over an hour.' All thoughts of Bella evaporated like dew in the morning sun. Mum stirred and pushed her eye mask above her head.

'Ah, morning, peanut.' She yawned and sat up, rubbing her eyes. 'It'll all be over soon.'

Willow nodded. She had been writing like a demon

but the steam had instantly run out of her fingers. Her head was all of a sudden screening the top-selling movie of Willow's nightmares: needles, blood, extractions. She felt fear grip her throat and she wanted to gag. Try as she might, she couldn't think of a desert island. Where was it when she needed it most?

'Oh, you've gone white! What's wrong?'

'I'm scared, Mum.' And she burst into tears. 'What if I don't wake up? What if they put the needles in the wrong place?'

'Peanut! None of that is going to happen. Come on, let's try a visualization . . . ' Mum got out of bed and sat on the bed with Willow and grabbed her hand. But Willow was shaking and sobbing. Her fear had gripped her and she couldn't shake it.

'I can't see the desert island, Mum. It isn't there in my head. I can just see . . . eww, all the neeeedles . . . ' And she started hyperventilating and crying at the same time. Mum held her really tight, at a loss for what she could do to help. Just then Anthony walked in, carrying two coffees. He hurriedly put them down on the bedside table and knelt down next to Willow and her mum.

'What's the matter?' he asked, all concerned.

'I think she's having a panic attack.' Lizzy had woken up now and was watching with a worried look on her face. She pressed the red button by her bed. A moment later a nurse walked briskly into the ward and looked at Lizzy, who pointed at the commotion, redirecting her to Willow's bed.

'What's going on here?' the nurse asked, whose badge told them all she was called Faye.

'My daughter is stressing about her extraction later on,' Mum explained. 'She has a phobia about needles. Dr Angelico has been helping her with it.'

'Ah, one of those phobias.' The nurse winked at Willow. 'We can't have you in this state if you're going to donate. Do you know I used to have a phobia about blood? How ridiculous for a nurse to be scared of blood! I couldn't even say the word 'blood'. I would want to pass out.'

Willow stopped crying and looked at Faye. 'Why did you become a nurse then?'

'Because I had always wanted to be one.'

'But what about the phobia?' Willow was intrigued now. Surely she was making this up?

'I had to have hypnotherapy. It worked because here I am!'

'And you don't mind blood now?'

'Not at all. I use the techniques I learned for all sorts of stresses now. My special place is a waterfall from where I grew up in the countryside.' Faye smiled. Her voice had soothed Willow's panic and jolted her out of the flashing images of needles and blood. 'Why don't you just lie down now, put the laptop away, and listen to your iPod? You've got about an hour before we take you down. Try to rest and imagine your special place. Mum and Dad can help by staying calm too and everyone talk quietly.'

'Thank you, Faye,' Willow's mum said gratefully. 'Come on, peanut, laptop away.'

Willow folded it over and placed it on the bedside cabinet next to the coffees.

'I'm so sorry, again, Willow, that this is such a stress for you.' Anthony looked stressed and in need of some calming techniques himself. 'I'll make it up to you somehow.'

Willow put her headphones on and lay back against the pillows. Anthony and her mum continued to chat and drink their coffee. Willow thought back to what Faye had said. She had mentioned her special place was a waterfall from home. Maybe she should try a special place from home instead of the desert island, Willow wondered. She closed her eyes and thought of home. Maybe she should be clicking her heels together in ruby slippers? Her special place was definitely the back garden in the summer. She loved it out there, chilling with Stella and Jarvis under the canopy of the apple tree and then eating dinner al fresco on summer evenings with the twins and their family and Mum, glasses clinking and laughter drifting out across the flowers and grass. She loved the smell of the jasmine trailing over the back walls of the cottage tingling her nostrils as she pushed her bare feet into the sun-warmed grass. While the birds tweeted in the summer breeze, the far-off rumble of tractors in the fields reminded you there were other people alive outside the confines of the crumbling garden walls. Yes, this was her special place all right. And before she knew it, she had passed an hour dreaming of home. Anthony had gone and Faye was there, telling her it was time. Time to donate her bone marrow to Bella.

'I'm just popping to the loo,' Mum said, already changed into clothes and raring to go. 'Hang on!' Faye busied herself with unclipping the wheels of the bed to make it into a trolley so Willow could be rolled down to theatre.

Willow felt anxious. Lizzy looked over from the bed opposite. 'Good luck,' she said. 'I think what you're doing is amazing, doubly amazing because of your phobia.'

'Thanks.' Willow smiled weakly.

'Your sister's very lucky to have you. None of my family was a match. She must be so happy you're helping.'

Willow nodded. What else could she do? She had no idea what Bella thought, apart from hating her.

Mum bolted out of the loo and Faye and the orderly rolled the bed out of the ward. Lizzy waved. But Willow was in her back garden at home, playing chess with Jarvis. She didn't see anything. All she knew was that it was a hot summer's day and she wanted some of Mum's homemade lemonade . . .

Chapter Twenty-eight
Bella takes a peek

Bella stared at the telly some more; she had no energy for anything else. Her dad had just come back from visiting Willow. She wondered what they had talked about. Had they talked about all the things they were going to do together in the future? Willow *had* a future, a secure one, one in which she wasn't going to have to re-grow her hair back with the possibility that it might grow back curly. One in which she wasn't going to have to have tests all the time to make sure the disease was permanently destroyed and would never come back. She would be able to have children if she wanted in her future. Having children was the last thing Bella wanted, only being eleven, but she had been told it was now something she could probably never do, not have her own children, anyway.

Bella's eyes stung with tears, jealous thoughts running through her head like the drugs coursing through her body. She couldn't feel anything other than rubbish. Talking to her psychologist hadn't really helped. She felt so closed up, so tight, that the anger burned deep down, using up her reserves of anything she might have left after her body had been blasted by chemicals.

'How are you feeling, darling?' her dad asked her. Bella had come round to actually talking to him after that weekend visit from Willow, but she was still offhand, still upset with him for everything.

'Tired.' She didn't want to talk and blinked her tears away. Being visited yesterday by Willow had made her feel even more rubbish; it had highlighted her baldness, her paleness, and her general sick demeanour. And accidentally seeing Willow the other week up here looking so smug and healthy had made her want to never see her again

Everything hurt. Her mouth was so sore that sometimes talking was an effort. And you could forget eating. Now she was in isolation from the rest of the ward, no kids could visit her, not even her brother. Her mum and dad could, and medical staff, but that was it. Everyone else had to stay behind the glass in case they brought in an army of germs that could attack her defenceless immune system. Her best friend, Pippa, had been to visit and it had made her miss her so much, and long for a normal day where they could hang out in the garden or her bedroom, laughing about nothing, or go to the cinema. Just doing everyday stuff that she wouldn't have thought twice about before now seemed like an exotic dream.

Bella thought about what her therapist had said about the bags of bone marrow, and how they contained her new life. She hadn't seen her bags yet; Willow was donating today. She was going to have part of Willow inside her bones. But, no matter how hard she tried, Bella just couldn't feel happy about it at all . . .

Time dragged . . . Bella was feeling fidgety but had no energy to do anything about it. And even if she had had the energy there was nowhere to go. Anthony was reading something on his iPad and looked totally engrossed. Bella kept trying to watch the film on TV but she felt too sick and her mouth hurt as though she had burned it on hot chocolate, except it wasn't anything as nice as that. This was so boring. The film was boring. Who cared about this girlie drivel? In any case she was sick of reading. All the books she'd brought with her were dull. Nothing caught her interest. Her laptop lay untouched in its case next to the bed.

After a while Anthony looked up and caught her looking at him. 'Do you mind if I go and get a cup of tea?' he asked her. 'I won't be long.'

She shook her head. Anthony kissed her nose and put his iPad down on the bed. Bella glanced at the screen. Anthony hadn't closed it down and Bella saw the title of what he was reading: *My Life: What Happens Next?*. Bella picked the iPad up and scanned the page. It was a blog. Not just any blog; it was Willow's blog! It was dated today and the entry was very short. Why would she want to read a blog written by Willow, the golden child? It would only be about how great her life was, how many millions of friends she had, how many parties she went to, how many ponies she had. Oh, whatever! Bella inwardly raged, staring defiantly at the iPad.

Every time she thought about Willow she wanted to scream. If she hadn't got this illness, Willow wouldn't be here and Bella wouldn't know about her and she wouldn't be in her life, ruining everything. Bella didn't want a sister. Especially not one who was going to save her life. That meant she would have to be nice and she didn't want to be nice. She could feel the anger like a hard black lump of coal sitting inside her, deep, deep down where no one else could feel it apart from her. Dr Collins, her child psychologist, had tried to coax it out of her and had done all she could to get her to open up, but she hadn't been successful. Bella had kept it locked up inside her inner core.

Bella was at odds with herself. Part of her had wanted to refuse to have Willow's bone marrow and die, just to spite them all, but then she thought about it. If she died then Willow would jump right into her shoes, might get her room at home, and might even make Archie like her, like a proper sister. Bella's head had whirred and whirred playing out all the scenarios until she couldn't think any more.

And to cap it all, Willow could write. Like her dad. Bella couldn't write, not really creatively, anyway. She could kick her way out of a paper bag and elegantly style out her moves in taekwondo, but not right now. Right now all she was good at was being ill. She put the iPad down but two words caught her eye. 'Secret sister' in a paragraph jumped out. So she read.

Sitting here, waiting for the time when I will have to be put to sleep, is like waiting for the knock on the jail door. For the hangman to come and get me. I imagine this is what it's like when you know you have to face the ultimate fear—your own mortality. Only my fears are paltry compared to that. I feel sort of OK now. The hospital is still under the Sleeping Beauty spell and I am the lone servant awake in a huge palace, writing away like a scribe recording the doings of the day. The only doing today is my biggest fear—an operation. For some reason, I cannot find it in me to recall the desert island I need to float away to, to be free of the sickness and the possible fainting. But imagine I am B. Now that opens up a huge can of worms. The sick princess in the tower who sees me as an interloper rather than someone sent to save her. I can't make her change her mind, make her see I will never, ever try and steal her dad from her. I have my own life and family miles away from them all. I love my life just as it is. But she must feel so dreadful. I know I represent all the things she isn't at the moment. I am well; she isn't. I can only imagine how desperate it must feel to have someone swing into your life and proclaim to be your secret sister. I would be terrified she was going to steal my dad away and feel jealous that she would be more popular than me, more interesting, more talented, more everything. That it would encroach on my family. If only she could see it's not like that. I wish I could reach her, tell her, reassure her: I just want to help. No dad-stealing will take place on my watch . . .

Chapter Twenty-Nine
Icebreaker

'What time is it?' Willow croaked. 'When's the operation?'

Her mum, who was sitting down next to her, took her right hand and patted it. 'The operation's over. You're back on the ward.'

'Oh. How come I don't remember anything? That guy put the mask over my face and then I'm here.'

'That's how anaesthetic works, peanut. You go to sleep and then wake up immediately, but you were out for a few hours.'

'I didn't have any nightmares!'

'I told you that you wouldn't!'

'What's that on my hand?' Willow lifted her head and looked at the bandage over her left hand.

'That's the cannula.'

'A needle?' Mum nodded. 'Eww.' Willow lay her head back down and sighed. She was actually too fuzzy-headed and exhausted to be bothered with the fact that a needle was piercing her skin. In real life she would have been having an epic-style fit by now.

'How do you feel?'

'Tired. And my back hurts a bit.'

'How's the heroine of the hour?' Anthony said as he breezed in the ward and stopped at the head of the bed.

'Fine.'

From behind his back he produced a beautiful wicker basket decorated with pink and white gingham ribbon. Arranged inside were a load of muffins, all with different-coloured icing and sprinkles on.

'Wow!' Willow said through her dozy state. 'Who are they from?'

'From us. Maria made them. They're the best muffins in the world. But then again, I'm biased.' He plonked the basket down on the table and he handed Willow a big white A4 envelope. She opened it and pulled out a homemade card. It was from Archie. He had drawn a picture of Willow with a light sabre, fighting what looked like a baddie. Underneath it said: *Princess Willow fighting off Darth Anaemia*. Inside he had simply written: *Thank you for helping my sister. Love Archie*. Willow felt choked up.

'Archie did the card all by himself. He wanted you to know that.' Willow smiled. She tried not to feel the cannula in her hand or imagine the puncture wounds in her back. And right now she just wanted to be in her bed at home. But she though of Bella. She can't go home, a little voice said in her head. She actually wanted to see Bella but right now what she wanted most was not to have to talk and to sleep . . .

The next day it was time for Willow to go home.

'Can we swing by and see Bella?' she asked her mum as they left the ward. She felt different now. She had done her job and somehow any animosity that Bella might throw at her didn't matter any more.

'Sure thing. I think she's getting your bone marrow today.'

So they wandered round to where she was. Willow and Mum looked through the glass and Bella lay motionless on the bed in her grey tracksuit. She had a blood bag next to the bed hanging on a stand and a central line going into her collarbone.

'You OK?' Mum asked, knowing Willow would find all the blood and lines distressing.

Willow had gone a bit green, but took some deep breaths. She didn't look at the blood bag; she just concentrated on Bella's face. She looked grey, like her tracksuit. And she was asleep, or she had her eyes closed at least. Anthony looked up and waved, mouthing bye at them. He had had a hug and goodbye from Willow earlier in the ward.

'Bye,' Willow whispered to them both. See you at the weekend, she thought. Anthony was visiting and taking her and the twins out for afternoon tea.

The tea was amazing in this super posh country-manor-type place near where our school is. I could get used to eating like this! Though I think I ate my own weight in egg and cress sandwiches and mini scones and was feeling like a turkey at Christmas.

When we got home and the twins disappeared down their drive A caught me off guard with something.

'I hope you don't mind but your mum and I need to have a chat with you. I'm coming in.' It sounded ominous.

'Er, OK,' I said. What could they want to talk about? Oh no, perhaps they have a secret son that they put up for adoption when they were at uni???? It wouldn't have surprised me one bit.

Mum was sitting at the kitchen table drinking coffee when we got in and we joined her.

'It's nothing bad, peanut,' Mum said, putting her hand on top of mine to silence my nervous tapping. 'We both just think that, now you know about your dad, maybe there should be some meeting times set in stone?'

'At the moment, nothing can be permanent because of B, but once she's out of hospital and well again, I can commit to regular meetings and maybe you could come up to town and stay the odd weekend?' A looked at me hopefully. But I felt . . . strange. That would never work...

'What is it?' Mum asked me, sensing something because I hadn't answered, I'd just shrugged.

'B doesn't like me. I don't want to stay at your house and it turn out all weird. What if she never likes me? Ever?'

'I don't know. I can talk to her. Make her see you're not going anywhere?'

'I know she won't like that. I wouldn't like that.'

'So what do you suggest?' Mum said.

'I don't know,' I said, because I didn't. I mean, how could the arch enemy somehow break down these impenetrable icy defences? What sort of olive branch was needed in a situation like this? But then I was suddenly hit by an idea and I couldn't believe I hadn't actually thought of it before! Maybe it would be just the icebreaker we needed . . .

Bella scrolled down. There wasn't any more. What icebreaker? Bella had been secretly reading *My Life: What Happens Next?* for the last few days. The blog had lots of followers. You could see who they were. Bella had noticed Stella and Jarvis were on the list and Stella had commented on a few posts—the ones mentioning her. She sounded funny. There was a picture of the twins at the side in the photo gallery. Jarvis looked so geeky it had made Bella laugh inside and she hadn't done that for a while.

The day she'd found Willow's previous post on her dad's iPad, she'd opened her laptop and searched for the blog online. Once she'd found it, she'd felt sick and not just from the drugs! It had felt like snooping, but it wasn't—it was a blog; people were meant to read them, weren't they? Bella hadn't known what to expect and as she'd read, the million knots in her stomach had begun to slowly untangle. It had been like reading a story and Bella loved reading books, but this had been better than a book. The feelings and thoughts were real and what was more 'parallel universe' was that it had been about her. Some of it, anyway.

It took Bella a few goes to read up to date that day because her mum was there, and she didn't want her to see what she was doing. And she kept feeling sick looking at the screen so much as well. But she wanted to keep reading more. She almost wished her mum would leave her for an hour or so just so she could read it without her asking what she was looking at. It was quite frustrating!

When she got to the bit about her being nasty to Willow she felt angry. Not at Willow for putting it in, but because of her own behaviour. Because, unknown to her, she was reading the Bella in the blog as a separate entity to herself the more she got into it. As though the people in it weren't her and Willow. She had distance from it. It had taken on the form of a fictional story almost. And she was upset with the Bella in the blog for being so mean to Willow who was only trying to help! Bella wanted to shake Bella! And that was the moment it clicked. She had a sister. *A blood sister*. Bella's eyes stung with tears. She really wanted the tale to have a happy ending . . .

So later on that day, as she lay on her bed wondering what to do with herself now she was up to date with the entire blog, she got a surprise.

'Bella, you had a parcel earlier.' Carrie, the nurse on duty, came in with it unwrapped. It had been through the antibac spray! Mum and Carrie watched as she looked at the book handed to her: *Little Women*. Bella opened it and inside Willow had written:

Dear Bella, I know you aren't happy that I am in your life, but I wanted you to know I'm not going to steal your dad away. I have my own life here with my mum and my friends. I just thought you might want to read a book that made me realize I wanted a bigger family, but most of all that I really wanted a sister before I even knew who you were. I hope you like it. I want you to get well. Love from Willow xxx

Bella smiled. Willow had mentioned this book in her blog. Now she had it in her hands. Maria asked to see. Bella looked up and was smiling, a real proper happy smile.

'Oh, my darling girl. I haven't seen you look so happy for ages!' And Maria promptly burst into tears. 'Sorry! I don't know what's wrong with me . . .'

'All perfectly normal!' Carrie said matter-of-factly and passed her a tissue. 'It's good to have a cry!'

'Look what she wrote, Mum.'

'Who?'

'Willow.' And Bella handed her the book.

Maria took it and opened at the title page and smiled. 'Oh, how lovely. I adored this book as a child.' And she burst into tears all over again.

Chapter Thirty
Little Women to the rescue

Mrs Bannister had called Willow aside after register at the end of that week to have a chat with her about her blog.

'No one has ever entered a blog for this writing competition before,' she said. 'But it's such a good idea. I can't see any reason why you can't enter it as it's still writing. There are ways we can work round it if it's not OK.' Then she stopped and asked something else. 'How's your sister doing?'

'She's OK, I think.' Though in truth, Willow didn't really know. She had sent the parcel two days ago. When she had had the idea, she had gone to the bookshop after school to buy the book and got a later bus back home. Mum had posted it for her. But since then she'd heard nothing.

'Well, I can't wait for the next instalment,' Mrs Bannister commented. 'My husband is reading it as well. You've sucked everyone in!'

Willow blushed. She hadn't updated her blog for the last couple of days or checked her emails. She felt that sending Bella *Little Women* was the last thing she was going to do. After that, she was stepping away.

When Willow got home that night she felt quite flat. The initial high she felt about sending the book had gone. She knew that if Bella didn't ever come round to the idea of having a sister it would make life very difficult for everyone. And how do you force the issue, especially with someone who had just gone through a massive trauma? Willow felt helpless.

She dragged her feet up the stairs into her room ignoring the wreck of the house and her Mum's trail of destruction in the kitchen. She chucked her school bag onto her bed. Her laptop stared at her from her desk. Come on, open me, you know you want to write something. Anything. There's nothing to write, Willow thought. I feel all written out. But maybe that's why you need to write, her inner voice said. Maybe you just need to flip the laptop open and log on to *My Life*. Just write what's in your head. It might cheer you up. But Willow felt there was nothing in her head apart from the sound of *meh*.

She sat down at the desk and switched on the laptop and waited for it to start up. Maybe writing would help with her funny mood before she popped round to see Stella. She logged on and noticed that she had a few more followers at the top of the page. One of the names looked familiar. *Bella J.* That must be Bella! It couldn't be anyone else. Willow's tummy did a flip. Her last post had comments at the bottom of it. From Bella J.

Dear Willow, thank you for the book. I got it yesterday evening. I have started reading already. I feel a bit better today. But my eyelashes and eyebrows have started to fall out ☹. Your blog is really good. I want to read what happens next. B x

Bella had agonized for ages about what to write. She knew she wanted to write something. She hadn't told her parents that she had written or had even read the blog. She didn't know what to say. Because deep down, in amongst all the anxiety about being so ill, her anger at the world for the unfairness of it, and feeling just so poorly, she felt stupid. After being so cross for so long, and aiming all that at Willow, Bella found it hard to take it all away again and be normal. She couldn't verbalize any of it; she was too tired. And saying sorry seemed so insignificant after what Willow had done for her. Especially taking into consideration her total fear of blood and needles. Bella herself had always found saying sorry really hard, even before she was unwell. For her it felt like a sign of defeat and acknowledging you were wrong, meaning you were weak. Bella was feisty and being wrong made her feel scratchy inside. But really, was there a wrong way to behave in a situation like this?

Reading the blog was also a sudden reality check. She had thought everyone was like her and had two parents at home, nice holidays, frequent visits to lovely places. Of course, she knew there were people with single parents and that not everyone was as lucky as her, but no one *she* knew was like that. But Willow wasn't poor and had a nice life; it was just very different to Bella's. Bella also realized that she would swap all the nice stuff just to be well again . . . She was tired of feeling so ill all the time. Every bit of her ached. She couldn't remember what it was like to just hang out with friends and be normal. Being in isolation was very boring—there were only so many DVDs, YouTube clips, or books to stop you going severely crazy. And no one talked about what would happen if she didn't recover . . . Reading Willow's blog had been the most exciting thing that had happened to her in ages . . .

B wrote to me! Look. Look at my last post—she said she liked it. At the bottom! Sending her *Little Women* must have worked. All the moody thoughts have packed their bags. There's nothing to say really. Other than get well, B, and I'm sorry your eyelashes and eyebrows have fallen out. I can't imagine how weird that is. We are all rooting for you. Everyone at school wants to know how you are. They are always asking me. People you have never met want you to get better. So you have to! That's all there is to it. I'm going to the twins' for tea now because Mum is in a meltdown about work and our house is like a living, evolving tip that could harbour its own ecosystem. I swear there could be rats foraging around the kitchen among the graveyard of dejected coffee cups and empty biscuit wrappers. We need a cleaner. Oh yes, silly me, I'm the cleaner! More exciting posts from the cottage in Weston buried under a heap of coffee cups as soon as we have an update.

Willow pressed 'post'. She felt happy. Just the fact of Bella liking the book and the blog lifted her mood completely. She told the twins and of course Stella had to log on immediately and check out what Bella had written for herself. And over analyse it, of course, being Stella! Sometimes words are just the words that are there with no hidden meaning. No matter how Stella looked at it, she had to admit defeat. 'I guess she wants to be friends,' was all she could come up with. Willow really hoped so . . .

Chapter Thirty-one
Blood sisters

Anthony rang after reading Willow's last post. 'Bella asked if you would come up at the weekend,' he said, sounding very excited. 'She loves that book you sent her. What a great idea, well done.'

'Thanks. I was just copying your idea . . . '

'One other thing: you can use our names in the blog. You're not a secret; people are going to find out I have another daughter at some point, so you may as well just use my name . . . I know you're not comfortable using the word "dad".'

Willow blushed. 'Er, thanks . . . What if the paparazzi come and break my door down and want interviews?'

'No one is that interested in me! Get over yourself! Ha ha.'

On Sunday Granna took Willow up to London because Mum was frantically trying to finish her sculpture in time for the cover-shoot deadline. They didn't need

247

Anthony to meet them in reception downstairs; they knew where they were going now. On the train on the way up Granna said, 'You know, I wouldn't be surprised if Bella makes a much speedier recovery now.'

'Why's that?' Willow asked.

'Because she's stopped being so angry. All the good energy can get to work now and heal her body. It's not fighting through all the anger first and exhausting itself.'

Willow looked at Granna as though she was crazy and she just raised one eyebrow at her, giving Willow the You Know I Am Right look. When she sat and thought about it maybe Granna was right. She was always right about weird stuff like that.

'Hello, Willow!' one of the receptionists said to her. 'Have you come to visit Bella?' Granna and Willow went straight to the outside of the room, where Anthony was hanging out with Archie, and Maria was inside with Bella. Bella was eating a banana. Willow couldn't really tell her eyebrows had fallen out because having no hair on her head made it seem perfectly normal for her eyebrows to be missing.

'Hello, Willow!' Archie said, his face beaming at her. He was holding a Lego *Star Wars* Millennium Falcon in his hands. 'Do you like this? It's my favourite thing ever in the whole world!'

'Looking good, Archie,' she replied.

'Hi, Willow!' Bella said shyly through the intercom. Willow noticed Maria and Anthony smiling at each other, a sort of knowing and relieved smile.

'I've got something to tell you. . .' Bella was grinning from ear to ear. Willow had never seen her smile before. She was still ever so slightly suspicious it was all a ruse and Bella would proclaim hatred at any second. But her smile made her look so pretty and happy, even without hair or eyebrows, that she dismissed the thought at once. 'It looks like your bone marrow has taken!'

'Oh, wow! That's such great news. When did you find out?'

'This morning, when they did their tests.' She carried on slowly eating her banana.

'Yes, the doctors are very pleased with her progress. Even in just a few days she seems to have improved massively, almost overnight,' Anthony said.

Willow looked at Granna and she winked at her. Granna should have her own witchy cable TV show because she just knew EVERYTHING! Willow thought.

'Do you want to stay and chat to Bella while I go

and take Archie for some lunch in the canteen?' asked Anthony. Willow nodded.

Granna looked at her wisely and said, 'I think I might come with you, if you don't mind.'

'Me too,' said Maria and made her way to the door out to the corridor. They were being abandoned. Willow wasn't stupid . . . When they had all disappeared and Bella had finished her banana Willow spoke.

'I'm glad you liked the book I sent you. I wasn't sure it was your sort of thing.'

'I love it. I've almost finished. The part where Beth gets ill is so awful . . . But Jo helps her pull through. I liked that part especially . . . '

'Yes, that was my favourite bit of the book too.'

'I love your blog more, though,' she said rather quietly. 'Because it's real.'

'Yes, maybe it's a bit too real. Sorry.' Willow apologized because she knew she had been very honest in it and Bella hadn't come off too well.

'Yes, but that's good. It made me see.'

'See?'

'That you had just as much of a shock as I did about Dad. That when you freaked out it took a lot for you to agree to donate. I didn't make it easy for you. That you have this horrible phobia—I can't believe you got through it at all. That you're normal and . . . nice.' Bella looked as though that bit was hard to say, that Willow was nice. Willow suspected that in Bella's head she had been the villain of the piece for so long that it was hard to break a habit of thinking in a certain way. 'I guess I'm trying to say sorry.'

'It's OK, honest.' Willow could tell Bella didn't do sorry!

Willow felt a bit awkward after that revelation, like she imagined you would feel if you went on a date with a boy and didn't know what to say next. Bella was sitting on her bed with her knees curled up in front of her and her arms wrapped around them to keep herself folded up. But she spoke first so Willow didn't have to.

'When I was first really ill and had to have all this time off school I missed out on a lot with my friends. And when I saw them at the house, when they came to visit, I felt so far away from them. They chatted about school, parties, all the stuff I used to get excited about. And I just couldn't get excited about it. I felt I wasn't a part of it any more.'

'Was that because you felt so ill?'

'No, not really. I did feel rubbish, but not like I feel now. I wasn't in pain or being sick. It was more they had no idea what I was feeling because they weren't ill. My best friend, Pippa, is the only one who really tried to understand. She offered to be tested as a match when we couldn't find a donor. She obviously wasn't.'

'That was really nice of her.'

'Yes, it was. And she has visited loads and written. She's my BFF for life, I think!'

'Like Stella and Jarvis for me. They're always there.'

Bella smiled. 'I feel like I know them. They sound funny.'

'They are. And so clever it makes my head hurt.'

'Maybe when I get home you and the twins could come and visit?'

'That would be cool. Thanks.'

'No, thank you . . . You saved my life.'

Willow shrugged. What do you say to that?

'Willow?'

'Yes.'

'I know you don't want to call Dad, "Dad", because . . . you know, everything that happened. But would you mind if we were . . . sisters?'

Willow felt a smile explode in her tummy and work its way up her entire body till it reached her face. 'Why would I mind? You *are* my sister!'

'And something else too. I felt it while I was reading your blog.'

'Yes?'

'I think you should change the name of the blog.'

'To what?'

'Blood Sisters.'

Willow nodded. She didn't need to think about it. It felt right.

And that was that . . .

Epilogue

'What time did they say they were coming?' Willow asked her mum for the millionth time.

'Calm down, peanut. They'll be here in time. Don't worry.'

'I am calm!'

'No you're not!' Stella said, standing next to her with her super-immaculate hair, ironed sundress, and white spaghetti sandals revealing perfectly painted neon-pink toenails. 'You look all mad and stare-y!'

'Thanks!' Willow sat down heavily at the kitchen table next to Jarvis, who squeezed her knee.

'The reporter and photographer aren't even here yet,' Mum reassured her.

Just then the doorbell went.

'Stay sitting, I'll get it . . . ' Mum said.

Willow could hear a female voice. It wasn't Anthony.

'It's Mrs Bannister,' her mum said.

'Hello, Willow. How are you feeling?'

'A bit sick, to be honest.'

'Don't worry about it. Just be yourself! We're all very proud of you, you know.' And she bent down and gave Willow a hug. 'I knew your blog would do something amazing.'

Mum busied herself getting glasses out of the

cupboard and lining them up on the work surface next to the fridge. The house was, for once, spotless. Outside in the garden a very long wooden table covered in white sheets stood incongruously amid fallen leaves and dappled sunlight. Mum had borrowed a table from next door to add to her own to stretch it, banquet-style. Thankfully the late September weather was shining gracefully on them so she was able to have the lunch party outside. Not everyone would fit inside her tiny house. The twins' parents had kept a lot of the food in their fridge next door and would join them later on with Granna.

'The doorbell!' Stella called to Mum, who scurried off to see who it was.

'Hey! Where's the star writer?' Anthony called from the hall. 'I need an autograph!'

He walked into the kitchen, carrying a huge bottle of champagne and a large white box tied up with tartan ribbon. Willow got up from the table and he gave her a bear hug. 'We're here!'

'Really? I would never have guessed,' Willow laughed.

Behind him followed Maria, looking as glamorous as ever, and then Bella and Archie. Mum introduced Mrs Bannister to everyone and they all shook hands.

Mrs Bannister seemed a bit overawed to be meeting Anthony and Maria, having confessed to being a fan of their books.

'Hi, Willow. Hi Stella, hi Jarvis!' Bella said shyly. Her hair had started to grow back. It was slightly lighter than before and still very short. The twins and Willow said hello. Archie had brought a new Lego *Star Wars* creation, still in its box, ready to make, and was already showing Jarvis.

'So, are you ready for the big interview?' Anthony said, clapping his hands together as Willow sat back down.

'Er, dunno.'

'Just don't say "No comment"!' Jarvis joked.

'But what if they start asking all the questions about you, Anthony? And don't want to talk about the competition?'

'*That's* when you say "No comment"!' He squatted down and took Willow's hands in his. 'There isn't anything they don't already know from reading the blog. You pretty much laid it out there, didn't you?' Willow nodded. 'So if they ask, just answer. If you don't want to answer, don't. It's as simple as that.'

Willow remembered back to the first morning of term more than three weeks before when Mrs Bannister had come into her new tutor group with a letter . . .

'Hello, everyone! Sorry to barge in here unannounced but I have some very exciting news.' Dramatic pause while everyone shuffled and pulled faces as if to say what could it be? 'Willow Fitzpatrick has been named as the runner-up in the New Young Writers' Competition run by *The Sunday Times* newspaper. Her blog, *Blood Sisters*, came second out of the whole country in the thirteen to sixteen category. She is the youngest person ever to have been placed so high up in the history of the competition. So, well done!'

Willow had sat there, totally overwhelmed while everyone started clapping. And then of course some of the cheeky members of the class asked if this meant they could have the rest of the day off to celebrate and wondered how much money she had won . . .

And here they were, nearly a month later, at Willow's cottage, waiting for a journalist and photographer from *The Sunday Times* to come and interview her and take pictures of her family and friends who starred in the blog. Of course, there had been a lot of media attention because it had come out that the father in the story was famous novelist Anthony Jerrard and that Willow was his secret daughter. The newspapers loved it! In fact, lots of people loved it. Her blog became the most popular blog on blogspot for a while until the next trend knocked it off the top slot.

'Hmm, not sure I like being overshadowed by the new girl in town!' Anthony had joked when Willow came to visit a week later. 'I'd better watch my back.'

'Maybe we'll be turned into a film?' Bella had said eagerly. 'I wonder who would play me . . . ?'

Willow had laughed. Bella was so different now, so bubbly and fun, but still with her steely core underneath it all. The two girls were definitely developing a sisterly bond that Willow had so longed for in her literary fantasy life of *Little Women*.

'Well, Brad Pitt would obviously play me!' Anthony had said.

'Dream on!' Willow had laughed.

Eventually *The Sunday Times* people arrived, interviewed Willow (no tricky questions), took their pictures, and headed on their way after having a glass of champagne. It turned out Anthony knew the photographer from way back and they had a good old chinwag.

Everyone was in the garden, milling about and chatting. Granna had just turned up, and the twins' family trooped through the shared garden gate with trays of food to lay on the mismatched set table.

Willow stood in the French doorway overlooking the autumnal garden and surveyed all the main players in her life, all of them cocooned in her special place— her back garden. In just over five months her family had doubled in size. All she had wanted was a family that stretched further than Mum, Granna, and her, and she had got so much more . . .

'So, did you get everything you wished for?' Granna said in her ear as she came up behind her and gave her a hug.

Willow turned round and looked at her open-mouthed.

'I'd close your mouth if I were you. You might catch a fly.'

'Granna! How do always know so much?'

'Because I'm old and wise. You'll get there one day.'

People were sitting down at the table. 'Come on, Willow, you have to sit in the middle, between me and Stella!' Bella called, pulling back a chair for her to sit on and giving her the most enormous grin. The sun caught her tufty hair, making it look almost red in places, and her eyes danced, full of laughter and sparkle, so different from a few months ago in the hospital when she was a shell of a person. She was almost back to her old self, but not quite, because she had experienced something so life-changing.

'Go on, pet. I think someone wants you,' Granna said, smiling.

Willow gave Granna a quick squeeze and skipped down the garden over to the table, pulling up her chair in between her sister and her best friend. She couldn't remember ever feeling this happy. She had got the bigger family she had dreamed about and she had had some success with her writing. In addition to everything else, she had faced down her crippling fear and now felt it wasn't going knock her sideways again in the future. And, to unexpectedly top it off, Mum had finally managed to magic two extra VIP tickets for the Lost and Found tour at Christmas. Stella was over the moon; neither of the girls had ever been to a concert before. It seemed Willow couldn't have come up with a more perfect ending than this, even if she had written it herself!

Acknowledgements

This book couldn't have happened without help from the following people. Simon Harper for putting me in touch with Doctor Pamphilon at NHS Blood and Transplant, Filton. Doctor Pamphilon suggested the exact disease I needed for the story to work! Also to Zoe Hayman for arranging my visit to the Royal Marsden NHS Foundation Trust in Surrey. Thanks to Louise Soanes at the Royal Marsden who answered all my questions on my visit, and afterwards on email. Finally thank you to Hannah Howard, a teenage cancer survivor, who told me what it was like to go through hell and come out the other side. I am indebted to you all for making the book as real as possible. There is dramatic licence taken in order for the story to work, but actual treatments and medical terminology are factually correct.

About the Author

Jess has worked as a book-seller, children's books editor, and DJ with her best friend (under the name, 'Whitney and Britney'). She spent her childhood making comics and filling notebooks with stories. Jess lives in London and draws constant inspiration from her three brilliant children!

How well have you remembered the 'Sister, Sister' story?

Why not try this quick quiz to find out . . .

 1. How does Willow find out about Anthony?

 2. What is the name of Bella's illness?

 3. Who first recommends *Little Women* to Willow?

 4. Who suggests Willow should write a blog?

5. What is the name of Willow's blog?

6. What was the name of Anthony's novel?

7. Whose party did Willow go to before her operation?

QUIZ ANSWERS!

1. Reading a letter he sent to her mum.

2. Aplastic anaemia.

3. Her class teacher, Mrs Bannister.

4. Anthony.

5. Trick question! At first Willow's blog is called 'My Life: What Happens Next', but she changes it to 'Blood Sisters' at the end of the story. Bonus point if you named both!

6. My Life in Smells.

7. Hattie's.

Writing Tips . . .

Do you love writing, just like Willow? Or do you find writing quite hard, but would love to get better at it? Either way, the best thing you can do is practise. Even your favourite authors have to work at their writing, to make it the best it can possibly be. So, where should you start?

1. *Don't be scared of making mistakes*
When you first start writing you don't have to show anybody if you don't want to, just write for yourself. Experiment with ideas and styles, and don't let worries about spelling and grammar stop you before you even begin. The important thing is to have fun getting your ideas down on the page. There's always time to edit it afterwards.

2. *Write about what you care about*
Do you have a hobby that you could tell people about? A band that you love, or a sports team that you support? It is much easier to write about a subject that you are passionate about, so once you feel confident enough to show people your writing why not create a newsletter or fanzine? You could make copies and give them out to your family and friends.

3. *Enter competitions*
Competitions can be a fantastic way to build confidence in your writing. Not just because you might win, but because it

gives you a purpose for your writing. Working hard on a story until you feel that it's good enough to enter for a competition feels brilliant!

There are lots of short story competitions that you can enter, such as the BBC's 500 Words competition. The rules are simple: you must be between 5 and 13 years old, your story must be no more than 500 words, and you must have permission from a parent, guardian, or teacher. The website, www.bbc.co.uk/500words, has all sorts of advice on how to begin.

4. *Get into the habit*
The more you write, the more you will want to write. You could start a diary, and write an entry every day. You could even set up a blog, like Willow, and update it regularly. Make sure you talk to a parent or guardian first, as they will have to manage the account for you if you are under 13.

5. *Read*
The best way to learn how to write is to read as much and as broadly as you can. Try to understand why you love certain books, and what you don't like about others. Get inspiration from other writers, keep practising, and eventually you will find your own voice.

And most of all, HAVE FUN!

MORE INFORMATION ABOUT Aplastic Anaemia

To find out more about Bella's condition, why not visit the AAT (Aplastic Anaemia Trust) website: www.theaat.org.uk.

The AAT is the only charity in the UK to focus solely on research on aplastic anaemia and support for all those affected by it. To date, the AAT has raised over £3million.

The AAT helps by funding research into the cause and treatment of aplastic anaemia, providing support and information to patients and their families, and raising public awareness of the disease.

DID YOU ENJOY READING
SISTER, SISTER?

Have you ever had to deal with any of the problems that the characters face in the story? And even if you haven't, how do you think you might cope in this situation, and what advice would you give to Willow?

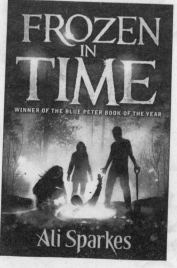